THE STREETS NEVER LET GO 2

**Lock Down Publications and Ca$h
Presents
THE STREETS NEVER LET GO 2
A Novel by *Robert Baptiste***

The Streets Never Let Go 2

Lock Down Publications
Po Box 944
Stockbridge, Ga 30281

Visit our website @
www.lockdownpublications.com

Copyright 2022 by Robert Baptiste
The Streets Never Let Go 2

Lock Down Publications
Like our page on Facebook: Lock Down Publications @
www.facebook.com/lockdownpublications.ldp

Book interior design by: **Shawn Walker**
Edited by: **Nuel Uyi**

Robert Baptiste

Stay Connected with Us!

Text **LOCKDOWN** to 22828 to stay up-to-date with new releases, sneak peaks, contests and more...
Thank you.

Submission Guideline.

Submit the first three chapters of your completed manuscript to ldpsubmissions@gmail.com, subject line: Your book's title. The manuscript must be in a .doc file and sent as an attachment. Document should be in Times New Roman, double spaced and in size 12 font. Also, provide your synopsis and full contact information. If sending multiple submissions, they must each be in a separate email.

Have a story but no way to send it electronically? You can still submit to LDP/Ca$h Presents. Send in the first three chapters, written or typed, of your completed manuscript to:

LDP: Submissions Dept
Po Box 944
Stockbridge, Ga 30281

DO NOT send original manuscript. Must be a duplicate.

Provide your synopsis and a cover letter containing your full contact information.

Thanks for considering LDP and Ca$h Presents.

Robert Baptiste

Chapter One

Kim

I was at work at Universal Hospital looking after the patient on my chart board.

When the paramedic rushed a gunshot victim in the hospital, it wasn't something that surprised me. I always see these young black males coming into the hospital shot up. This is what takes place in the city of New Orleans every night. Somebody getting shot up. This is why it's called the Murder Capital, so I did expect nothing else.

That's why I'm trying to get the fuck from down here. I'm trying to move to Atlanta. More black-owned business and less killing.

If I got pregnant, I wasn't going to raise a baby here. I don't give a fuck what Slim said. His ass can stay but as soon as they call me for this hospital job I'm gone.

As I rushed over to the body, my fucking head went to spinning; my heart went to pounding, beating against my chest. I started having shortness of breath.

What the fuck, I thought to myself.

"We got a victim with multiple gunshot wounds to the chest, arms and legs, and one to the head."

Fuck, I thought to myself, *this can't be real.*

This shit can be happening to me.

As I looked at Slim on the stretcher shot up, my head really went to pounding.

"His vitals are dropping. He about to crash."

Shit! The sound of the paramedic brought me back to reality.

I watched them perform CPR on him. He stopped breathing for a minute.

"Let me try." I pushed the paramedic out the way and went pressing on Slim's chest, giving him mouth-to-mouth.

"Come on, motherfucker, you better not die on me!" I said, crying and hitting on his chest.

Just then he started breathing again. They rushed him into surgery. I sat there a nervous wreck. My mind and thoughts were all over the place. My fucking worst nightmare was coming true. I got up, pacing back and forth, praying to God that he makes it through. Sharon came down the elevator. She works with me.

"Girl, I heard they brought Slim in."

"Yes."

"What they say?"

"Nothing yet."

"Damn! I'm sorry," she said, hugging me.

"See all this beef shit need to stop," I said, crying on her shoulders. I fell to my knees crying. Sharon helped me up and brought me to the chairs and rubbed my back.

"I feel you."

"This shit is becoming too much for me."

"I feel you. Trust me." Just then the doctor walked out.

"Morris family?"

"Me."

"Kim?"

"Yes. He's my boyfriend. How is he?"

"Lucky. The bullets went in and out. And the one that hit his head only grazed it. Good thing it was dark. Bad thing he's in a coma."

"Damn! Okay. When can I see him?"

"Give it a minute or so. He's just coming out of surgery."

"Okay, thank you, Doctor Warren."

"No problem."

"You want me to come with you?" said Sharon.

"No, I got this."

"Let me know if you need anything."

"Okay," I said, hugging her. I walked in the room. He was laying there with tubes running all over his body. I wanted to break down and cry. My knees got weak and I was fighting back the tears. But my heart was hurting seeing him like this. I walked over to him nervously, reaching out, touching his hand. I have seen people like this before in the hospital. But it never affected me like this. I guess when it hits home, shit is different. Then I rubbed his head and leaned in, kissing him.

"Come back to me," I said, with tears welling in my eyes.

I couldn't bear seeing him like this. So I walked out the room.

***

Tre

I woke up to my phone ringing. I looked at the clock; it was five in the morning.

I looked over at my side bitch—Michelle—out the Melpomene Project down the street from the Magnolia. I know I don't supposed to be back here. But this bitch got some fire head, pussy and asshole. Plus, the bitch down for a nigga. But this bitch keep asking me to leave my girl and come be with her and have a baby with her. It cool we fucking but I'm not leaving my girl for her.

The bitch is super thick, black as the Ace of Spades, with smooth chocolate skin that I love to rub on, and she got long wavy hair like an Indian. She's Creole and black mixed. I grabbed my phone off the dresser and looked at the number. It was my girl texting me with 911 behind her message for me to call her asap.

I raised up in a rush, picked up the phone, calling her back.

"What's going on!"

"Slim been shot."

"What! When?"

"I guess last night."

"How is he?"

"In a coma."

"What?"

"Yea, Kim there with him now."

"Okay. I'm going to hit her."

"Okay." After I hung up the phone, I called Kim.

Shit! Straight voicemail.

I sat on the edge of the bed with my head hurting, thinking.

I grabbed my clothes, threw them on, then grabbed my gun and headed out the door.

***

Len

I got out my bed walking to the door where somebody was banging on my shit. I 'm going to curse their ass out if it's not a matter of life or death.

"Who the fuck is it?" I screamed.

"Me Tamika." I want to know what her fat ass wanted. I hope this bitch wasn't trying to get weed from me because I was out. I yanked the door open fast with an attitude.

"What the fuck you want this early in the morning? I could have been getting me some dick."

"Well, I just want to let you know Slim got shot last night."

"What the fuck!" My knees buckled and I grabbed my chest, falling back in the door. It felt like I just got kicked in the chest by a horse. She helped me sit on the couch.

I couldn't even speak.

"Are you okay?"

"I need a cigarette." I took one out the pack, lighting it up, then took a long drag, pulling the smoke in and out my nose and mouth.

"Where he got shot?"

"In the Calliope."

"Is he dead?"

"I don't know."

"Damn! Fuck! I need to be by myself. Thanks for telling me." I slammed the door behind her. I paced over the floor. I picked the blunt out the ashtray, lighting it up, hitting it. My head was all fucked up. I couldn't even think.

A bitch had to go lay back down.

***

Tre

I had been riding around the city thinking about Slim. I called Kim but she never answered. Sent me to voicemail.

Fuck! My dog laid up in the hospital with bullet holes in him.

I'm going to find out which one of these pussy ass niggas took a hit on him. And I'm going to kill their ass.

I already think this pussy ass nigga out the nine ward named Real had took the hit on me and Slim. I had it on my mind to kill him anyway. I just couldn't find him.

Damn! This nigga got shot up in the Calliope. Why the fuck he was back there, knowing them niggas on the new side was beefing with them niggas!

Damn! Slim, you was tripping.

I pulled the blunt out the ashtray, hitting as I turned on Washington, going into the projects. I stepped out with my nine Glock under my arm. You can't trust no nigga or bitch out here in the city when you got money on your head.

Niggas you know from way back will kill your ass for the money we got on our heads. That's why I'm going to find out where this nigga Boo rest at and kill his ass.

I walked in the circle where all the fiends was lined up to get some dope. I had a couple ounces. I went to serving them with the gun under my arm. I made a quick stack on the morning rush. I stepped in the hallway and snorted me a bag of dope to get the money off my back.

I wonder if Len heard about Slim getting shot up last night. I'ma go holla at her after I finish bumping this dope.

"Tre, I need you gram," Bum said. I handed him two grams for six hundred dollars.

Bum was a nigga from across the river that score grams and sell bags over there. When I have weight, he come score too.

"Good looking out," he said, walking off.

As I was serving, Tamika came walking up the court way.

"What's up, Tre?"

"Nothing, coolin'."

"You better be careful. I seen the boy—Real—back there the other night looking for you and Slim. He the one that shot Slim car up."

"That's what's up. Good looking out. You know who they said shot him."

"I need a few dollars."

"How much?" This fat bitch be knowing everything, and she be on point with the shit.

"Two hundred." She walked in the court way. I handed her two hundred, and she whispered in my ear.

"Fuck no, I'm not going to believe that shit."

"Man, I'm telling you. You need to watch yourself. They got money on y'all head."

"Alright. Good looking out." Damn! I was fucked up by what she just told me. I had to take a seat on the porch. I had to snort me another bag of dope.

Fuck! This city in our throats for real! Motherfuckers do not care whether you're family or not.

I need to find out who set him up back there. 'Cause I am going to kill their ass too.

***

Murder

I pulled up to this bar in the lower ninth ward Cross the Canal. This where this nigga Boo be hanging. He found out through the street I took care of the business for him. I know this nigga Real was trying to take the hit, so I beat him to it. Real and I was fucking the same bitch out the Calliope named Poo. She told me the nigga had paid her five grand to set my uncle up, and I told the bitch I would give her ten grand if she let me know when the nigga made it her house.

I told her to tell the nigga Real too, because I was going to kill both of them niggas. Uncle or not, nigga, I got the $250,000 on your head. Your ass is out of here. Tre ass next. I already put my team on him. I told them whenever that nigga come in the project, *kill his ass*. They got $250,000 on his head.

I was going to Real because he got a lot of heads under his belt and got a nice rep in the city for killing. So, if I killed him, my rep gets bigger. Besides, hoes like niggas in the city that got a rep, a big dick and snort dope.

When I walked in the bar, a black bald guy walked up to me.

He went to patting me down. He grabbed my gun and popped the click out and the one in the chamber.

"Damn! Like that?" I walked up to Boo who was sitting at the table in the back corner smoking on a cigar.

"Have a seat."

"Where's the money?"

"You killed Slim, huh?"

"Yea, you owe me two hundred and fifty thousand dollars."

"I thought he was your uncle."

"Better me than somebody else. At least he will be in a casket looking sharp."

"Damn. Ain't no love in the city for real."

"This bitch ain't named *Cut-throat City* for nothing."

"Well, what about his friend Tre?"

"I'm on him right now."

"Well, you only get half the money since one of them still living."

"I thought it was two hundred and fifty thousand dollars on each of them."

"It's a quarter million for both of them. Now I can give you a brick of raw, or you can take the hundred and twenty-five thousand dollars in cash."

"Well, give me the brick of raw this time and next time I'm going to take the cash." He signaled to the lady behind the bar. She walked out with a brick of dope, wrapped it up in silver foil with a red stamp on it.

"Thanks."

"Finish the job."

"I'm on it."

"Oh, that bitch Poo ain't shit."

"You can't trust no hoe."

"That's how it is on the street."

He nodded and the guy gave my gun back.

"I need my clip."

"It will not happen. *Cut-throat City*. Remember."

"Later." I walked to my car, getting in, and popping another clip in my shit. I was on my way to the Magnolia to look for this nigga.

Chapter Two

Tre

I knocked at Len's door. She opened the door with her eyes bloodshot red.

"Damn! I'm sorry, Len," I said, hugging her.

"Is he dead?"

"I don't know. I been trying to holla at Kim, but she ain't answer her phone.

"Damn! That bitch ain't shit." We sat on her couch smoking weed.

"So what you heard on the streets?"

"Man, I don't know what to believe. So many niggas he was beefing with. Some people say it came from the beef with the 7th or some 9th ward shit."

"What you heard about his nephew?"

"Shit, they was talking like he took the hit."

"Damn! You think he would do that shit to Slim?"

"Money make a motherfucker do strange things."

"I know nigga will cut-throat your ass in a heartbeat."

"And you right. You can't trust a motherfucker in these streets."

"I know that right."

"Okay. Let me make a couple moves in the project to see and hear what I can."

"Okay, be safe."

"Later." I pulled up on the Magnolia driveway. I don't see none of them young niggas outside.

I rode down some more on LaSalle drive.

A nigga went to hitting at my car. I smashed out, heading out the project. When I pulled up on Claiborne by the pizza hut, I stepped out and noticed I had four bullets in my car door.

"Damn! Niggas getting at me. Alright, these niggas want war. I'm going to give it to them."

I jumped in my car, pulling off, heading home to get my chopper. These motherfuckers don't know who they fucking with. They must think I'm soft without Slim. These niggas crazy.

***

Murder

I pulled up on Magnolia driveway. They had police all over the projects.

"Damn! ain't a bitch! I wonder what happened." I stepped out the car, leaving the gun and brick of dope in there.

I ran upstairs knocking at the trap house door. Joe opened the door.

"Where the money?"

"I don't get it."

"What! They said—"

"Chill, niggas, I'm going to put us on. Why the police all back chere?"

"Shit, I got at the nigga Tre."

"You shot him or killed him."

"No."

"Damn! Now the niggas going to be on point."

"Man, we going to get that nigga!" Pepper said.

"What up with the nigga Slim?" Joe said.

"That nigga history." I looked out the window. The police were leaving.

I walked to the car, grabbed my gun and the brick and went back to the trap house. I sat on the table.

"This what the nigga gives." Me and my niggas—we broke it down to grams and H bags, and it was that fire we have the project on lock.

"I'm feeling that," Pepper said.

"Me too."

"Then the nigga said, if we killed this nigga Tre we get another hundred and twenty-five thousand dollars."

16

"Nigga, we gotta get on that lick," Joe said.

"And I'm trying to kill that nigga Real too."

***

Real

I pulled up to the bar. I stepped out with my .45 in my waist mad as a motherfucker.

"Man, what's up, Boo?"

"Wassup, Real?" Boo said.

"Man, what's good? How you going to put somebody on my lick."

"I told you I need that shit."

"Man, I was on the nigga. I had the hoe to set the nigga up in the Calliope. But when I made it there, the nigga was dead already."

"Well, you need to check that hoe. And don't come in this bitch like you running shit. You my man and I'm the boss in this motherfucker."

"A'ight. So what up?"

"His man still alive. It still a hundred and twenty-five thousand dollars out there."

"Who took the nigga out?"

"Some little nigga out his project named Murder."

"I know the little nigga."

"Okay."

"Later." I jumped back in my shit, snorting me a bag of dope before pulling off.

This bitch played on me. I know the bitch was fucking with the little nigga. She must have put the nigga on the lick. But why did she call me too? Unless the nigga was going to kill me too.

I'm going to kill that bitch and that nigga when I catch them down bad.

***

Robert Baptiste

Two Weeks Later

Tre

I pulled back up in the project around 6 o'clock. The sun was about to go down. I had holla at my other nigga in the project. He was down for that murder shit. I had couple hoes off the new side letting me know when they seen this nigga—Murder and his crew. I had found out that it was Joe—Murder's nigga—who shot at me.

I also found out through the streets that this nigga was the one who shot his uncle up. I thought Tamika was lying but then my real nigga from down the way told me this nigga Boo paid Murder a brick for doing the shit and the $125,000 on my head when the job is done. So you know I'm about to fuck these little niggas up.

I jumped out the car with my chopper in my hand and a banana clip that held 75 rounds. I walked up the court way going into the hallway.

Craig walked up with his chopper. I walked into the hallway.

Craig was my partner from way back. He just don't hang with us. He be doing his own thing. But when it come to this beef shit with the other side, he with the bullshit because a nigga from the other side of the projects killed his little brother.

He killed the nigga and went to sixty days back town, and they dropped the charges because they don't have no witness to the case.

So he always down to kill one of the them niggas.

"So, nigga, what happened?" he asked, hitting a bag of dope.

"Man, them little niggas shot at me today. Call themselves taking the hit for this nigga Boo from out the nine ward. And this nigga Murder shot up Slim."

"I thought Slim was the nigga uncle."

"Nigga, money turn your family into your worst enemy."

"Damn! I see it's time to get rid of these niggas if they rockin' like that."

"Nigga, I'm with that," I said, cocking my handler back on the gun.

***

Murder

I sat on the porch in the Magnolia projects in the Magnolia Courtway with my crew smoking on a blunt of purp. I was dressed in black Girbaud jeans, a white wife beater and some black Reeboks, talking to my niggas. We had the choppers stashed in the grass and one in the hallway just in case this nigga Tre comes trying to creep on a nigga. We started pumping the dope I had got from Boo; that shit was that gas. I had my side of the projects sold up. Niggas and hoes was coming from everywhere to score dope. My name was ringing in the city from the murder job I pulled off with Slim.

"Nigga, we got this shit pumping out chere," Joe said,

"I told you niggas I was going to put us on," I said, passing the blunt.

"This dope got our pocket sitting nice in just a couple weeks," Pepper said, hitting the blunt.

"That's up with you, nigga," Ant said.

Ant was one of my crew members. He really wasn't about the gun play but the nigga could hustle like a motherfucker. He was short and black with wavy hair. He just came home from Juvy a couple months ago.

"Chilling getting this money," Pepper said.

"I ain't seen that nigga Tre around since I hit at him," Joe said.

"You know that nigga ain't shit without Soulja," I said,

"Murder, let me get three for the sixty," dope-fiend Ray said.

"Here you go."

"Good looking."

"Let me get the same," Rena said.

"Here you go."

As I stood up, I saw Craig and Tre spin the bend busting, with two choppers in their hands.

"Oh shit!" I said, ducking in the hallway.

Boom! Boom! Boom! Boom! Boom! Boom! It sounded like thunder being struck.

My partner, Pepper, jumped in the hallway with me, grabbed the chopper and went to hitting back. Joe jumped behind the dumper. Ant tried to run, but got shot in the head and back. We went to exchanging fire until the police started pulling up, jumping out of their cars. We went to hitting at them, making them jump back in their cars and pulling off out the projects.

Craig and Tre ran through the cut. We went upstairs to the dope and out the back driveway and jumped in our car, pulling out the projects.

"Damn! Them motherfuckin niggas killed my partner," I said, hitting the interstate .

***

Tre

Craig and I broke through the cut going to the Willow Courtway. As we was coming through the cut, we saw Len on the porch. We ran upstairs to her apartment, going inside.

"Boy! What the fuck! What's wrong with y'all?" she said, coming inside, looking at us trying to catch our breath.

"Shit! The police was running behind us," I said.

"What y'all do?"

"Trying to kill this nigga—Murder—and his crew."

"Y'all get him?"

"No. We killed one of his niggas."

"I wish y'all would have killed his ass."

"Believe me, I'm on the job. Him and this nigga, Real. You know where that bitch Poo be hanging at?

"No, I really don't know that bitch, but she be hanging in the Calliope."

"Shit can go back there. Nigga beef with them."

"You heard from Kim?" she asked.

"No."

20

"So is he dead or not?"

"I can't tell you that because Kim ain't answering her phone."

"Damn! This bitch is down bad for that shit."

"Let me try to call her now." I picked up my phone, dialing her number.

"Shit! Straight to voicemail."

Robert Baptiste

Chapter Three

Two Months Later

December 1996

Kim

I sat in the hospital room with my head on Slim's hand while he was sleeping.

When my phone started vibrating, I looked at it. I saw it was Tre.

I sent the phone to voicemail.

I don't want to have nothing to do with nothing. I hoped no one thought I had something to do with Slim being in a coma or getting shot.

I felt that one of the reasons he was in a coma was because he was fucking around with Tre and all this beefing and robbing they do together. I don't just blame *him*. I blame Slim ass too, but right now I don't want to be bothered with him.

Word on the street says he's dead. As long as people may believe that, I don't have to worry about a motherfucker coming into the hospital and trying to kill him.

I heard that Slim and Tre have a lot of money on their heads.

Slim been getting serious threats in the hospital too.

When he get right, I'm going to tell him to go lay low by his cousin in Texas. At least until he heals up.

It's been a couple months he's been in a coma. I'm hoping he comes out.

Lord knows I need some dick. Plus a bitch is lonely as hell out here. Niggas been trying to holla but I don't have time for that shit.

As I lay my head back on his hand, I thought I was tripping when I felt his finger flinch. But then it moved again. I jumped up running, going to call the nurse.

"Somebody come help me!" I screamed.

The nurse came running into the room.

"What's wrong?" she asked.

"His finger just moved." She watched his hand and it moved again.

She rushed out calling the doctor.

A few minutes later, a white, older doctor walked in wearing a white coat.

"Glad to see you back, Mr. Morrison." Slim just looked at him, pointing to the tubes in his mouth.

"Okay, I'm going to pull them out in a minute. But first tell me if you can feel this. Blink two times." As the doctor rubbed his gloved hand on each foot, he blinked two times.

"What does that mean, Doctor?" I asked.

"That means he's not paralyzed."

"Thank you, Jesus," I said, throwing my hands in the air.

"Now say 'Ahh'."

"Ahh!" I watched as the doctor moved the tubes out of his throat. Then the nurse removed the tubes out of his dick.

"W-w-w—" He was trying to say something.

"You want some water?" I asked.

He nodded. I walked to the bathroom and put water in his cup. I held the straw so he could drink it.

"Thank you," he said.

"I miss you, baby," I said, with tears running down my face.

He slowly moved his hand to my face, wiping the tears away.

"I love you."

"I love you," I said, kissing him on his dry lips.

The nurse walked into the room.

"We got to take you to the X-ray room to make sure everything is alright with you."

A few hours later, the nurse brought him back to the room.

"He's good now, but we are going to keep him a couple more days just to make sure."

"Okay." I smiled.

"You miss me?" he said.

"Nigga, I was going crazy as fuck without you. Don't scare me like that no more."

"I'm sorry, I won't."

"You promise?"

"Yes." I leaned over, giving him a hug and kiss. He grabbed my ass.

"Bae, stop. We in the hospital."

"I ain't had none in two months."

"The first thing you do when you come out a coma is want some ass."

"Hell yea."

"You *sad; straight tripping.*" I smiled at him.

***

Len

I sat on the porch in the Magnolia hustling ten-dollar bags of weed as I smoked on a blunt.

"What's up, Len? You got something?" Toya said.

"Yea, what you want?"

"A dime bag."

I walked in the hallway, grabbed the dime bag of weed and handed it to her.

"Let's smoke something."

Toya was light-skinned with tattoos on her neck. She was slim with green short hair, a cute face and nice size titties. Plus the hoe like me. She goes both ways.

"Come on." We walked in my apartment. She sat down on the couch, rolling the blunt as I went and put the weed up. I came back and sat on the couch as she passed the weed to me.

"Bitch, it's hot in here."

"I know. I already told the maintenance people to come fix my A/C."

"I'm about to take my shirt off." She pulled her shirt off and I looked at her pretty titties and red nipples.

"Bitch, you sure got nice titties," I said.

"You see my tattoo?"

"Bitch, I see that heart. That bitch is *live*."

"Bitch, I heard about Slim."

"Yea, bitch. Shit crazy in New Orleans."

"I know right."

We smoked the blunt in silence. Then we looked at each other with lust in our eyes.

She slid over to me, tongue-kissing me. I rubbed on her nipples as she rubbed between my legs. Then she pulled my shorts off and went down on me on the couch.

"I been wanting to eat this pussy," she said, then went to licking on my clit. I had a couple hoes eat my pussy before, but never returned the favor. I let them hoes eat me out and I came all in their faces.

I need to relieve some stress anyway.

"Fuck! Yea, eat this pussy, bitch!" I said, grinding in her face as I came back to back.

Damn, this bitch can eat some pussy.

***

Slim

I sat up in the bed looking at the nurse changing my bandages.

"Baby, does it hurt?" Kim asked.

"No. I'm just sore as a motherfucker."

"Oh."

"So, Ms. Nurse, when can I leave the hospital?"

"Well, soon as the doctor clear you." I looked over at her name tag and it read: *Texas*.

"Texas. What the fuck!" I said, looking at Kim.

"Babe."

"Why am I in Texas?"

"Can you excuse us? I am a nurse. I can change his bandages," I said.

"Okay. I'll be back," the nurse replied.

"I'm listening," Slim said.

26

"Well, the night you got shot you died, but I brought you back. It was a miracle you came back. Then you went in a coma. While you was in the hospital, you was getting death threats. People were about coming to kill you in the hospital, so I called your cousin. I got him here so he could help protect you."

"So people think I'm dead, huh?"

"You got shot four times—two in the chest, one in the arm and legs, and you got grazed in the head."

"Well, I'm not staying in Texas. Nigga not running me from my fucking city."

"Slim, we need to think about moving."

"*You* need to think about moving."

"What! You mean after I cried all these months over your ass. And you want to go back to that shit."

"Baby, the people I robbed ain't going to stop. Plus I'm on probation. They going to have a warrant on me. And my nigga Tre in the city by himself going through this shit. I can't just leave him to die. I would be a bitch ass nigga for that."

"But they think you dead."

"Look, I'm not going to leave him fucked up out there to fight a war."

"So what about me?"

"It's going to be alright, I promise you that."

"How? If your ass in a box—"

"It's going to be okay."

"What the fuck ever, Slim!" she said, walking out the room crying.

Robert Baptiste

Chapter Four

Poo

Smoking a blunt, I was sitting on the porch in the Calliope talking to one of my best friends—Regina.

"Bitch, you know the word on the street is that you set Slim up?"

"Yea, fuck the streets. Them bitches and niggas and hoes say anything."

"Well, bitch, you know you still got to be careful. These niggas don't give a fuck about no nigga or bitch. Anybody can get it."

"Fuck the streets. Here." I passed her the blunt.

"Bitch, there goes Real."

"Fuck!" I watched as Real pulled up to the driveway. I hope this nigga don't find out I was trying to get him killed for Murder. Murder is my baby. And Slim. I just be playing on Real cause he pops a bitch off.

He jumped out his F150 with his gun in his hand walking up to me fast. My heart was about to jump out my chest. I know this nigga don't give a fuck about killing no bitch. But I had to play it off; I could show no fear.

"Hey, baby!" I said, smiling.

"Come inside, let me holla at you?"

"For what?"

"Bitch, bring your ass inside."

"I'm going to be right back," I said to Regina. As soon as I stepped inside, his backhand hit my face and I fell on the couch, holding the right side of my face.

"Bitch! Why you ain't tell you was fucking with this nigga Murder?"

"Ain't nobody fucking with no Murder."

"Bitch, don't lie to me?" he said, hitting me again.

I grabbed my face again. "Nigga, ain't nobody lying to you."

"Then how in the fuck he knows Slim was in the projects."

"He gave me and Regina a ride and we saw him back chere."

"Bitch, you a lying hoe." He slapped me again, making me fall back on the couch. Then he jumped on me and started choking me.

I kneed him in the nuts and jumped up running into the kitchen, grabbing a knife. I ran back in the living room trying to stab his ass. But he ran out of my house. I ran behind him as he ran and jumped in his truck. He knew I was not playing with his ass.

"Bitch, I'm going to kill your ass if I find out you are lying."

"Bitch ass nigga, fuck you. Get out the fucking truck!" I said, with the knife in my hand.

"Chill, Poo," Regina said, grabbing my arm.

"Let me go." I pulled away from her, picking up a bottle off the ground and threw it at his truck. He stopped, jumped out with his gun in his hand. I stood in the middle of the driveway with the knife in my hand.

"Nigga, what? Fuck you."

"Bitch, you lucky," he said, looking around at all the people outside.

He jumped back in his truck, pulling off.

"Girl, what happened?"

"That bitch put his hands on me. And I don't play that shit. I'm not one of them weak bitches. I wish Murder would have killed his punk ass. Fuck that nigga."

"Bitch, why he hit you?"

"Talkin' about I should've told him I was fucking Murder."

"Bitch, he found out?"

"Yea, some bitch ass nigga or hoe told him."

"Damn! That crazy."

"Fuck that nigga. I need a blunt. Let's go smoke."

Chapter Five

March 1997

Slim

It had been six months since I had been out the hospital. I had been ducked off at my cousin's house in Houston, Texas. I been trying to let myself heal up before I went back to the city and find out who shot me up so I could kill their fucking ass. I know I probably had a bench warrant out for my arrest because I hadn't reported to my parole officer. Fuck him! I got bigger problems than me going back to prison. Like getting back to the city to help my nigga fight this war, and my fucking record deal.

Shit! Hope I still have one.

My girl Kim been coming to see me from time to time. She wanted me to stay out here in Texas, but ain't nobody running Soulja Slim of my fucking city. Fuck that! I'm not no bitch ass nigga. I'm from the Magnolia. All we do is breed souljas.

But I been chilling by my cousin with plenty of hoes and drug to use.

I got out the bed still sore. I walked to the bathroom to take a piss. When I finished, I walked in the room, looked at the fine ass Spanish bitch with long black hair and a phat ass I smashed last night on them X pills my cousin introduced me to. Them bitch is good. I don't know if they on them motherfuckas back home; they need to be.

I looked at myself in the mirror, seeing the five bullet holes in my chest, arms, legs and the scar in my head where the bullet grazed me.

Good thing it was dark, and the nigga couldn't see good, because he would have blown my fucking head off. The Lord was with my black ass because the bullets that hit my body went in and out. Not hitting major parts.

Damn! I need to get rid of this morning sickness and get back to hustling.

I walked downstairs looking for my cousin. I spotted him outside in the backyard by the pool on the phone with a couple naked bitches walking around.

I walked outside and saw a tray of drugs with pills: dope—coke. I took the straw and hit a line of dope, killing my morning sickness.

"What's up, cuz?" he said.

"Coolin, killing this morning sickness."

"I see. You liked last night."

"Yea, the shit was off the chain."

"Man, you need me to put some money behind you with this rap thing."

"Na, I'm good." My cousin was a big-time drug dealer who made a lot of money from real estate. I don't need him in my pocket on this rap shit. Because he the type of nigga that want to control shit. And to niggas like that it ain't going to make it.

"Well, I'm about to dip back to the city."

"Okay. If you need help with anything, holla at me."

"Well, I need to use that truck to get back to the city."

"You can have the Tahoe."

"Good looking out."

"Look, if you get your money right, holla at me. I got some nice prices on some bricks of heroin. China white."

"Okay, Wootay, I'm out." I snorted another line, grabbed some of the X pills for the road, then dapped him off.

"Love you, cuz," I said, hugging him.

"Love you too. Be safe." I jumped in the truck, smashing out.

***

Slim

I left my cousin's home and made it back to the city in about four and a half hours.

A nigga like me was tired of being duck off. A nigga like me is about that life and if it's going to happen, I welcome it.

As I came through the Kenner exit, I picked up the phone dialing Tre's number. I was trying to see what the fucking business is. I had a .38 I took from my cousin, but I needed something with at least fifteen shots.

"Who this?"

"Me, nigga."

"Slim? Soulja muthafucking Slim?"

"Nigga, you best know it."

"Nigga, I thought it was over."

"Nigga, you know they can't kill a soulja. I got nine lives like a cat."

"Where you at?"

"On my way in the city. Where you at?"

"Riding around looking for this nigga Murder or Real."

"Murder—my nephew?"

"Yea."

"What! Na, let him live."

"Man, your nephew did some fuck up business."

"Man, I'm sure whatever it is—it can be worked out."

"Nigga, we got a lot to discuss."

"Okay, meet in the projecst. And I need me a tool."

"I got you."

"Later." As I rode in the city, my head was all fucked up. My nephew and my best friend! Damn, this shit's fucked up. A nigga out the game for a minute and shit goes fucking left.

"Shit! Fuck!" I pulled up in the project about thirty minutes later. I jumped out the Chevy Tahoe my cousin gave me. I really don't like the car but fuck it! I need something to get around in.

Tre pulled up in a silver Cadillac Seville and stepped out with his gun in waist. We walked up to each other.

"What's up, my nigga? I'm glad to see you back."

"Yea, you know they can't keep a good nigga down."

"Here—the Glock," he said, handing it to me.

"Let's go in the hallway. What's good?"

"Them niggas and your nephew from the new side be coming here shooting at niggas on the old side."

"Come, let's go in my apartment." When we walked in, I walked to the back making sure nobody was in there in the project. If niggas or dope fiends don't see somebody using the apartment, they'd think it was abandoned and used for a smoke house or a dope house.

We sat at the table rolling something to smoke.

"Nigga, do you got some dope?" I asked.

"Ya." He slid me a bag.

I snorted the whole thing.

"Tell me what's going on."

"Man, your nephew took the hit on you and me. He the one that shot you up."

"What! Stop playing."

"Man, I'm telling you. Got the dope pumping, and everything on the news."

"Damn! This little nigga do me like that? Family."

"Man the fuck up!"

"Who the fuck can you trust? So, what up with this nigga Real?

"He took the hit too."

"Where he at?"

"I don't know. I'm on a mission looking for him."

"Okay. So this nigga Boo the one got the money on our heads?"

"Yea."

"We got to kill his ass and Real and Murder, and whoever want smoke."

"We need a lick for real. I been getting a couple ounces. But nothing major."

"Okay, I'm on it," I said, hitting the 51335.

"Okay."

"What up with my hoes—Len!"

"Dyking with that slim pretty bitch. Toya."

"Oh yea. I need to go holla at her."

"A'ight, nigga. Later," he said, dapping me off.

"Later." I ran upstairs knocking on her door. When she opened the door, she almost fell out. She broke down crying, giving me a hug and tongue-kissing me.

"Baby, I miss you so much. Let me look at you. You look damn good."

"I do."

"Fucking right. Do the dick still work."

"Yea, you want to try it out?"

"Fucking right. It's long overdue." She led me to the bedroom, took off her clothes as I took off mine. She fell on the bed spreading her legs. I slid my dick in her soaking wet pussy, putting her legs on my shoulder, driving deeper into her pussy walls as she grabbed me. I pulled her close to me, and she dug her nails into my back, tongue-kissing me.

"Fuck! I miss this dicks," she moaned.

I drove my dick deeper and deeper into her as she came all over my dick. Her pussy was so good and felt so sweet.

"Fuck, this pussy good." She got on top of me, riding my dick, biting down on her lip, shaking, and coming.

I grabbed her ass cheeks, slamming her down hard on my dick as I came all in her pussy.

"Fuck! I need that, daddy." I got up, putting on my clothes.

"You leaving already."

"Yea, I got a lot of shit to straighten out in the city."

"Okay. Please come back."

"I got you." I grabbed my gun and walked out the house.

I jumped in my car, pulling off. I picked up the phone, calling Bond.

"What's good?" he said.

"Man, what's good?"

"Slim?"

"Yea."

"Man, I thought you was dead."

"No, but have you seen my nephew? Is he there with you?"

"Yea, he just left from over here a couple of minutes ago."

"Yea, I'm going to kill his ass."

"Man, I heard."

"Look, I'm going to check up with you in a couple days

"Okay. I need to holla at you anyway."

"Okay. Later."

***

Death

I laid on the bench in the backyard at the dope house in the 8th ward on St. Rock, getting a cross in the middle of my forehead. I already had two black teardrops in my face. From putting in work.

My crew was the *8th Ward Animals*. Niggas know when I come it's lights out. That's how I got my name: Death.

"You finish, my nigga?" Tee said.

I got up, took the mirror from him and looked at it. I just killed a nigga in the 6th ward. He had ten stacks on his head.

Just then my nigga—Gray—pulled up in his truck, bumping this nigga Soulja Slim shit.

I walked from the back yard, getting in his truck.

"Nigga, turn that fuck nigga shit off."

"Damn! My nigga, you get fuck up every time you hear this nigga. Why you be hating on him?"

"Hate on him? I'm not a hater."

"So, what's the problem?" Gray and I go way back to first grade. We started this *8th Ward Animal* shit together.

"Man, I never told you this nigga was the one that killed my mother back in the day."

"What!"

"Yea, him and his man ran in the house and jack my mother for a key of coke and killed her."

"Damn! My nigga, I'm sorry to hear that. Why you never told me?"

"Just something I want to keep to myself. But if I ever catch that nigga down back, I'm going to kill his ass."

"We going to kill him," he said, throwing his CD out the car.

***

Slim

I pulled up to Kim's apartment in Slidell. She don't even know I came back to the city. I'd seen her car, so I knew she was there. I need to call my mother too.

I knocked at the door.

"Who is it?" she said.

"Me."

She opened the door with her belly getting bigger and still had an attitude. She was still mad at me because I don't want to move or stay in Texas.

"I see you made it back, huh?"

"Man, you should chill with the bullshit."

"This not bullshit."

"What you want me to do? Stay in a city where I'm not comfortable."

"I want you to stay your ass alive so you can see your daughter born."

"I am. I am."

"We going to see."

"Damn! Like that?"

"You don't care, so why should I? I'm tired of crying over you."

"Okay, let me get some of my clothes and I'm out." I walked to the room with her on my heels.

"You not going nowhere."

"Man, don't start that shit."

She took my clothes out of my hand. "I'm serious. Watch out."

"No." I grabbed her arms and pinned her on the wall.

"Chill out," I said.

"Fuck! No."

She went to trying to fight me.

I spun her around, pulled her panties off, bent her over and slid my dick into her wet pussy.

"Stop! Get off me." I slid deeper inside of her.

"Stop! Stop! Please don't stop!" she said, slowly backing up on me.

I held her by the waist, slowly riding her as she moaned, pushing back on me.

"Fuck! I'm about to nut."

"Yes, shoot it all in me. I love you, Slim."

"I love you too." I shot my hot nut all in her pussy as she came all over my dick.

**

Murder

As I was on my way to the projects, my phone rang.

"Hello," I said,

"Nigga, you know this nigga alive or not, huh?"

"Man Jo, what the fuck you talking about?"

"Nigga, my bitch just seen this nigga come out Len house."

"What? That hoe might be tripping."

"Man, I tell you."

"Okay, nigga, I'm on the way. Later."

Man, what the fuck! I put like five holes in this nigga and shot this nigga in the head. What the fuck! This nigga got nine lives.

"Ain't this a bitch." My phone rang again.

"What up, Poo?"

"This nigga Real just came back chere slapping me up asking me about you and Slim."

"What the nigga said?"

"That I tried to set him up for you and Slim?"

"And what you said?"

"Nothing. But you got to watch it. I think the nigga is trying to put it together."

"Okay, keep me posted."

"Okay. You coming to get me?"

"Yea, I got to handle this nigga saying this nigga ain't dead."

"Who?"

"Soulja Slim."

"What! You ain't killed this nigga?"

"Man, I shot this nigga a thousand times." Just then my phone beeped.

"This is Boo."

"What's good, Boo?"

"Man, why I'm hearing your uncle still alive?"

"I don't know. But I'm on it."

"Well, you owe me, and you haven't killed his friend yet. You need to be getting on this shit."

"I'm on it."

He hung up.

I pulled up in the projects in my Lexus. As I stepped out, my bitch—Coco—walked up to me. Coco was my other bitch who stayed on La Salle. She held all my dope and guns. She was short, black, and ugly but the bitch got some good pussy, ass and head. I heard she been fucking young thug niggas in the projects.

"You heard that nigga back, huh?"

"I heard." I walked in her apartment, sitting down at the kitchen table where they had a couple dope bags and money. I pushed the money through the machine and snorted a couple bags of dope. Then my crew came in the house.

"What's up, nigga?" they said, dapping me off.

"Nothing."

"How you want to handle this shit?"

"Shit, we going to kill them niggas."

"We need to score some dope. We out."

"Okay, I'ma hit Keedy up out the Melp. He got that fire. He got the Melp bumping with the dope."

"Okay."

"I'm about to go to the studio and finish this album."

"Later, nigga."

"Babe, you coming back here later on?" Coco asked.

"Yea, you know I gotta come get some of that fire." I grabbed my Mac, heading out the door.

Robert Baptiste

Chapter Six

Real

I pulled up in the St. Thomas projects in the 10th ward. A nigga got to be careful back here 'cause these niggas about jacking and killing you back here.

I jumped out my truck, ran upstairs in a dark hallway with my Mac out, knocking on the door of my bitch—Wanda— as I kept looking up and down the hallway, making sure no nigga was trying to creep up on me.

"Who is it?"

"Me."

She opened the door with nothing on but a see-through teddy.

Wanda was my main bitch. She was light brown-skinned, about 5'4 with short brown hair. She be holding guns and stuff for me. Sometimes she'd stash dope when I jack them niggas for it. All she fucks with is head busting niggas. She used to fuck with Slim back in the game.

"Nigga, what took you so long? I'm horny as shit."

"I been trying to take care of some business." She led me to the room, helped me take off my clothes and proceeded to drop to her knees, giving me head. She deep-throated it and sucked on my balls like a pro. She raised up, getting on her knees as I got behind her slamming my dick in her from the back while I grabbed her by the neck, choking her. *This bitch likes it rough. This is how she gets off.*

"Yes, keep slamming the big fucking dick into my pussy, motherfucker!" she said, looking at herself in the mirror.

I slammed my dick in and out of her soaking wet pussy as she came all over my dick.

"Fuck! Yea, give it to me. Shove that dick in my asshole." I pulled out of her pussy and shoved in her wet asshole that feel wetter than her pussy, fucking the shit of her. She gripped the sheets, telling me how much she loved me.

"Fuck! I love you."

"Bitch, you better." I started to shake.

"I'm about to nut!" She pulled my dick out her ass, sucking on it until I came all in her mouth, and she swallowed every drop.

I laid back on the bed, trying to catch my breath as she went to the bathroom. Just then my phone rang.

"Whooo."

"Nigga, you know this nigga still alive?" Boo said.

"What! That's what you get for fucking with that fuck nigga—Murder."

"Look, take care of all of them. I got two hundred and fifty thousand dollars, plus a brick of heroin for you."

"I got it handled."

"Later." I jumped up, putting my pants on.

"Where you going? You just got here."

I kissed her lips. "I gotta go get paid."

"Be safe."

***

Slim

I sat in the studio talking to Bond and Mike, smoking on a blunt of purp load on heroin with a .40 sitting on my lap. I really came over here to catch my nephew so I could put two in his head and get him out of my way.

"Man, I'm glad your ass is back," Mike said. "Nigga, I thought you was dead."

"Na, they can't kill a real nigga. What's up with the deal?" I asked, blowing the smoke out my nose.

"Bad news. Hype dropped you when they heard you got killed."

"What about the contact? You call and tell them I'm still alive."

"I'm going to see what I can do."

"Damn! I guess a nigga back to grinding at square one, you understand me?"

"Yea, because I don't think they going to re-sign you with all this street shit going on. They just don't wanna invest their money in somebody they feel not going to be around."

"Fuck it."

"Well, I'ma try to get you some concrete to put some money in your pocket."

"Yea, I need some."

"But you got to chill."

"Man, I'm a street nigga. I told you that before. Now that I got shot, it's on for real.I'm going to kill my nephew and the rest of the crew."

"He on my label," Mike said.

"Well, you need to get you a new rapper because *he* is dead."

"Like that, Slim?"

"You know me. Real nigga. You cut-throat me for the outside off the top, then you got to go."

"I feel you."

"You going to try to work on another album," Bond said.

"Yea, I'm going to get my name back out there. I got a couple raps in my head. I might lay a few here and there, but it's not going to make me focus."

"Okay, let me know something."

"I'm going to let you know. I got to get studio money first."

"Okay, holla later at me and let me know something."

"I'm out."

"Later."

Robert Baptiste

Chapter Seven

Tre

As I was standing at the gas station pumping gas in my car on Napoleon and Claiborne Ave., I saw a black SUV truck spin in the gas station. I got spooked and grabbed my gun off my waist. The next thing I know—Real and some niggas jumped out busting at me. I hit back, ducking behind my car. As I was busting at one nigga, another nigga came around busting at me. I ran toward the store and caught a bullet in the arm that pushed me through the door.

I fell on the floor and slid down one of the aisles. The nigga went to busting into the store, shooting the cashier. They was about to come in the door until they heard the police siren coming. Never thought I would be so glad to hear that sound.

I stumbled to my feet, looked at the cashier dead from the gunshots to the body and head.

I stumbled out of the store and ran to my car. I saw the police cars pulling up to the gas station in my rear view. I thought they were going to come behind me. I ducked off on a side street, pulling into somebody's driveway.

I wrapped my bandanna around my arm tightly, trying to stop the bleeding.

I waited a minute then I pulled off. I pulled up to my girl's house in the East. Sharon just had moved out there.

I knocked at her door. When she opened it up, I fell on the floor.

"Boy, what the fuck happen! Where did you get shot?"

"In my arm." She helped me up, bringing me to the bathroom. She grabbed a couple towels to stop the bleeding. I knew she knew what she was doing. She was a RN just like Slim's girl. As a matter of fact, they were best friends, but I didn't meet her through Slim's girl. I met her at the jail house. I was fighting a murder charge and she was a nurse. I had known her from way back in the day. We went to junior high school, but I never holla at her. But when she saw me in the Old Parish, we went to kick it. She went to bring me stuff: food, dope, and a cell phone. We even fucked a couple times in there. She was holding a nigga down for the two years I was fighting the charge. I beat the charge and came home, then moved in with her. And we been together ever since.

She been holding all my money.

Sharon is caramel-skinned, 5'6 and fat-fine; that means she in between thick and fat. She wore her blue hair short.

"You need to go to the hospital."

"Na, man, I'm good. The bullet went straight through. Just bandage me up."

"You sure?"

"Yea." She took my clothes off and helped me get in the shower, running the water over my body, making sure I don't have no more blood on me. Then she poured peroxide on my wound and bandaged me up.

"Boy, your ass gotta chill with this beef shit."

I felt weak. She helped me to the bed where I passed out.

***

Slim

As I was sitting in the studio smoking a blunt and listening to a new beat Mike just sent to me, I was trying to write some lyrics to the beat. Just then my phone rang.

"Wootay," I said.

"Man, them nigga out the 9th ward try to kill me

"Who?

"Real and his crew."

"What the fuck! "

"Yea, them nigga shot me too."

"Okay. We going to ride on them nigga. I know where this nigga hangs at.

"Okay. I'm in the project already.

"I'm on my way."

Click.

"Man, I got to go take care of some business."

"Man, how you expect to get back nationwide and you stay in some street shit?" Bond asked.

"Man, look, this street shit is part of my life. This rap shit come second. Remember that." I walked out and jumped in my truck, smashing out.

I pulled up in the project. Tre was already there waiting on me. He jumped in the truck with two choppers as we pulled off.

"How you feeling?" I asked. He shot a bag of dope in his arm.

"I feel good now." I pulled my needle out the glove box, shooting it in my arm as well.

"Let's ride "

We spun the corner on Forstall Cross the Canal in the lower nine ward, where these niggas be hustling at. We spotted them niggas hanging out this dope house on the porch smoking and selling dope.

"I got this," Tre said, rolling down his window.

Tre hung out the window busting with the chopper at them. Niggas and hoes went to screaming and running. I jumped out busting. I shot one nigga in the head and shot a bitch in the leg. Tre ran behind Real, shooting him in the back. I watched as he fell to the ground. Tre ran over to him, shooting him in the face and body. I saw the police hit the corner and I let off a couple shots to back them up.

We jumped in the truck, smashing out the neighborhood.

We jumped on the Claiborne Bridge, heading back uptown.

"Now that's how the fuck you take care of business," Tre said.

"Yea, I over killed the fuck nigga. He should have finished me."

"I like how you did that."

"This nigga Boo is next."

"For sure. I got an old bitch down that way. She can give us the low on the nigga."

"Yea, do that shit. His ass is next on the hit list."

"I just made a rap out that shit."

"What!"

"Nigga, it's going to be called *Soulja Life*."

"I like that shit. Fire."

"Where you going?"
"To my girl house."
I dropped him off and headed to the studio.

Chapter Eight

Tre

I pulled up in the Melpomene projects a couple of months later. I had healed good, and heroin helped a nigga with the pain. My side bitch—Michelle—been crying about me not spending time with her. I jumped out my truck with the .45 in hand, running up to her apartment at one in the morning. Knowing I'm tripping for being back chere, I stuck the key in the door, and she was sitting on the couch in the living room watching reruns of *Martin*, smoking on a blunt.

I sat on the couch next to her as she passed me the blunt. I been messing with her about a year now. I had met her at the second line across from the Magnolia projects.

She stayed in the Melp by herself with no kids. Pretty slim yellow bone with short green hair and nice titties and a cute round ass. She knows I got a girl.

That is why she be on my neck about me leaving her. She stays asking me all the time when I'm leaving my girl. Like I always tell her, I'm not leaving my girl. *You're my side piece. When you decide to leave, go ahead, you free*. But she never does.

As I was hitting the blunt, she unzipped my pants and started giving me head on the couch. I grabbed her head, moving up and down on my dick as she swallowed it. She sucked on my balls and my dick head until I came in her mouth.

She grabbed me by the hand, leading to the bedroom, taking off her blue boy shorts and her halter top. I dropped my pants and shirt to the floor and climbed on top of her, inserting my 8-inch dick into her wet-warm pussy.

I put her legs on my shoulders and started fucking the shit out of her as she dug her nails into my back, telling me how much she love me.

"Fuck! Daddy, I love you," she said, coming with her body shaking.

I flipped her over, slamming my dick into her pussy as she grabbed the pillow screaming while her pussy started making the farting sound as a result of her cumming and being so wet.

She laid on her stomach as I grinded my dick deeper into her as she came some more all over my dick.

"Fuck! I'm coming again." She squeezed her legs tighter as I slammed deeper and harder into her while I started shaking, coming, shooting all my hot nut in her pussy.

"Fuck! That was good, baby," she said, laying her head on my chest as we laid in our come, soaked in sweat.

Just then my phone rang.

"Woo, nigga. What happened?"

"I got a lick for us."

"Okay, come scoop me up."

"Where you at?"

"In the Melp."

"You still fuck with that babe, huh?"

"You know real niggas going to do them."

"Okay. I'm on the way."

"Later."

***

Slim

I pulled up in the Melp spooking. Hope a nigga ain't shoot my truck up. Tre came running out the dark hallway with his .45 in his hand, jumping in my truck.

"What you got?"

"A nigga in the eleventh ward."

"Who that be like?"

"Nut."

"Okay. I heard the nigga was playing with a couple keys of coke."

"Yea, he a old bitch ass, a nigga I been wanting to get from back in the day on stunt and rep hunting."

"Fuck, you know I'm with the bullshit."

"Yea, I need a couple g's in my life."

"Shit, me too."

"I got to pay for this studio time."

"I feel you." We pulled up to this nigga's house across the street from Shoe Town. We got out the truck and ran up to the door.

"Man, I don't see the nigga Lexus," I said.

"Okay, let's go in." I kicked the nigga door open as we ran through the nigga house. I ran straight to his room as Tre reached the kitchen.

I went through the nigga closet, finding some money in a shoe box. I flipped over the mattress and found a Glock. I went through the nigga's draws and found some rings and watches.

"Nigga, I found a half key in the tide box." We searched the house for another fifteen minutes and then left.

"Nigga, I'm about to go try and fuck one of these freaks of mine."

"Okay, my nigga. Drop me off in the brick."

"A'ight."

"What we going to do about this nigga Boo?"

"I'm going to hit this bitch."

"Do that."

"I'm on it." I pulled up in the 'jects.

"Nigga, hold the stuff. I'm going to fuck with you in the morning on it." I picked up the phone as I smoked on the weed, dialing this bitch Peaches' number.

"Shit. Voicemail."

"Look, bitch, this Slim. Hit me back when you get this. It's important."

I went inside and laid out the half brick of coke. I pulled some out of it, making a few bags so I could sell and snort.

I walked downstairs and sat on the steps, sat on them, snorting a line of coke and lighting up a blunt, taking a hit.

Just then Craig walked up.

"What's up, nigga? What you doing out chere?" he asked.

Shit coolin'. Trying to catch sells."

"What you up to?"

"On a flight trying to get off this dope bags."

"I heard that."

"Yea, nigga trying to put some money in my pocket."

"For sure."

"Yea, man, I heard them niggas out the nine ward trying to get the money."

Yea, bitch ass nigga Boo. He got some money on a nigga head."

"What y'all did like that? Y'all ran in a nigga spot and jack him?"

"For sure."

"Y'all need to take me with y'all on some of them lick."

"Nigga, you gotta be around."

"Let me hit that?" I passed him the blunt, watching him hitting it.

"Nigga, you know where some lick at?" I asked.

"Hell yea."

"Where?"

"They got this quarter shop in mid-city 24/7."

"Let's go on a jack move."

"Shit, let's do it."

As I was riding around, my phone rang. It was my bitch out the Desire. Peaches. She was my throwback pussy. I know this bitch know the low downtown body, everything and everybody.

"Woo. What's up, bitch?"

"Nothing. Nigga, I thought you was dead."

"No, bitch, let your nigga do the think for you."

These are the type of hoes you got to handle or the bitch think you weak.

"What up then, daddy?"

"Bitch, I need you to let a nigga slide through. I need to ask you a few things."

"Okay. Come over."

"Bitch, you ain't got no nigga slid up through that motherfucker?"

"Nigga, you know all I fuck with is sugar daddy."

52

"Alright, I'm on the way." I pulled up in the Desire project in the dark driveway. I jumped out with my gun in my hand, running into the dark hallway as she waited for me with the door open.

In this motherfucker you got be on your toes; these niggas back here really do not care. This motherfucking project is the worst in New Orleans for real.

She had on a red thong and white wife beater, with her hair hanging to her shoulders freshly permed. Peaches is an older bitch that fuck with nothing but sugar daddy, and loved that coke and weed, and sometime do a little dope every now and then. I met her back in the day when I used to come back here and score dope.

The bitch knew who I was and was all over my dick. At first I thought the hoes was trying to set me up because she was so aggressive about me coming back here in her project. It scared me. But I came and the bitch let me fuck her all kind of ways. And we smoked and chilled after that. I been fucking her ever since.

"What's good?"

"Nigga, you brought me something, plus dick?" I threw the gram on the table. She opened it up, making a line and took a dollar, rolling it up, snorting a line.

I took the needle out my pocket, shooting it in my vein.

"I see you move up, huh?"

"Bitch, go get me some weed," I said, lighting the hump up, letting the dope hit me as I blew the smoke out my nose.

We sat in her bedroom, smoking weed and high off dope. She went down on me, pulling my dick out, sucking on it for a minute. She sucked on my balls and deep-throated me for a minute. Then she pulled her thong off, climbing on top of me.

I laid back in the bed, letting her ride me like a horse as she dug her nails into my chest, shaking as she came all over my dick.

I gripped her ass cheeks, slamming her down on my rock-hard dick as I finger-fucked her asshole.

"Damn! Nigga, a bitch coming again," she said, bouncing up and down.

I flipped her over in a doggy style position, fucking the shit out of her as her pussy went making a fart sound. Then I laid her on the side, slamming my dick in her from the side as she held onto my neck. I'm not going to lie—the bitch got some good pussy and asshole. She slid my dick out her pussy into her asshole, slamming back on me. She rose up, getting on her knees as I thrusted out of her while she grabbed the pillow screaming my name as she came back to back.

"Fuck! Fuck! I'm coming, you big motherfucker."

"I'm about to nut." She pulled me out her asshole and turned around, letting me shoot come all over her face. Then she sucked on it.

"Fuck, nigga, I miss you."

I fell back on the bed as she got up and went into the bathroom.

She came back out, got in the bed, and grabbed the blunt out my hand, puffing on it.

"So, where this nigga Boo be hanging?"

"He hanging around this hole-in-the-wall bar where I work at."

"Good."

"I heard he got a lot of money on your head."

"Yea, the bitch ass nigga got me shot up."

"I see," she said, rubbing her hands over my bullet wounds.

"Yea, my nephew took the hit."

"What! Your family."

"Yea, this how family do you."

"Motherfucking money."

"Yea."

"I'm just glad you not dead."

"Me too."

She laughed. "So when you going to put out some more new music?"

"I'm working on something right now."

"That's good. You need to force on that shit and stay out them mother-fucking jail houses."

"Might as well be going back. I ain't check in with my P.O."

"Well, let me give you some of this chocolate pussy before you go back."

"I thank you for the pictures and money."

"I got you." She climbed back on my dick and began riding me again.

***

Slim

We sat at Len's house in the kitchen, counting the money. It was ten grand. And a half key. The jewelry looked like it could be worth something.

"Damn! I thought this nigga was on. The way he be flossing in the club."

"We grabbed his ass and made him bring us where the keys was at. I don't think the bitch ass nigga got shit."

"He might just be nothing but a stunt ass nigga."

"That's why a lot of niggas get kidnapped in the city stunting for bitches like they playing with keys, knowing they might not be getting nothing but a half of key or a whole keys."

"That's how fake niggas do. Then have a nigga like me on their line."

"Here goes 5 and 4 1/2."

"Well, this keep the chef off me until I find another lick to hit."

"You want some of this jewelry money."

"Yea, just holla at me when you get it." Just then my phone rang.

I looked down at it and it was Kim. She had been blowing me up for the last couple days. Between the dope, hoes and the studio, I ain't been home in couple days. I been staying in that old house in the Magnolia or by Len shit.

"Who that?" Len asked.

"Kim."

"Well, answer the motherfucker," she said, passing the blunt.

"I know I'm about to hear a lot of bullshit."

"You sure is," Tre said.

"Woo!" I said to Kim on the phone.

"Nigga, don't *woo* me. You must be out your fucking mind."

"I'm on my way home." I hung up the phone.

"Man, I'm out," Tre said.

"Me too," I said, kissing Len.

***

When I walked in the apartment, Kim came running up to me fussing like she always do.

"Where the fuck you been?" I been calling you all last night. For the last couple days. I thought you was dead. Slim, I'm getting tired of this shit."

"Man, look, stop sweating a nigga. This why I won't move in here with your ass."

"Stop sweating you?"

I walked off from her, going into the room, taking off my clothes.

"You must been fucking some of them hoes."

"Na, Tre got shot a couple nights ago."

"I heard. Sharon called me. That's why I been calling you."

"Well, I had to take care of that shit."

"I'm sorry about Tre."

"It's cool." I know once I hit her with the shit about Tre, she was going to get off me fucking hoes. Which I'm tired of her talking about. I been getting tired of her ass and been thinking about leaving her ass alone anyway. She been on this baby and getting married shit. And complaining about me getting high and shit. I jumped in the shower, letting the hot water rinse the pussy smell off my dick. I was thinking about this bitch Peaches, how she let a nigga fuck her all in the asshole then pulled it out and suck the come out my dick. See the type of bitch I like. With no limits. Kim better get her fucking mind right or I'm out this bitch. I ain't got time coming to this bitch every night with that fussing shit. I got too much shit on my mind to be putting up with fuck shit.

***

Slim

Two Weeks Later

Tre and I sat outside this bar room across the street from the Desire projects waiting on this nigga Boo to come out. I couldn't believe this nigga was getting all this money in the city and hang out in a hole-in-the-wall bar.

But the bitch Peaches told me this where the nigga grow up at in the Desire projects; this is how the niggas back here still with fire dope. He be supplying them niggas. My bitch told me he's in there with one of his partners.

"What's taking this nigga so long?" Tre said, hitting the hump.

"Chill, nigga," I said, hitting blunt.

"Nigga, it feel like we been out two hours."

"It's cool."

"I'm real to smoke this nigga."

"Okay, we going to give it twenty more minutes."

"Nigga, I'm ready to go in that motherfucker and shoot up everybody," Tre said, pulling the chopper off the back seat.

"Chill, nigga. They on the way." Just then my phone rang.

"Hello."

"They about to come out. Now."

"Okay."

"What she say?"

"They on their way."

"Okay."

"There they ass go right there with two bitches."

"It's on." We jumped out the car creeping between some cars. As they were about to get in his car, we ran up on them shooting them up. I shot his partner, hitting all in the head and body. The hoes went to screaming. Tre shot Boo all in his face and body. We shot them nigga twenty times apiece. We left blood everywhere, even all over us. We jumped in the car, smashing out.

We sat on the porch steps smoking on a blunt loaded off dope.

"Man, you seen that nigga face," Tre said.

"Yea, bitch ass nigga thought he couldn't be touch."

"Nigga, sure his ass was touched. You know we did," Tre said, giving me a fist pound.

"Nigga, I'm about to get in here and fuck this bitch Len."

"Okay, I'ma go fuck this hoe—Kelly—in the next hallway."

"Later. I'll get up with you."

"Later," he said, dapping me off.

Chapter Nine

Murder

"Roll something up, bitch," I said.

"Nigga, don't call me no bitch!" Poo said.

"You my bitch," I said, leaning over, kissing her.

"You right," she said.

She looked in the glove box, pulled the plastic bag out full of weed and stuffed some in a cigar. She rolled it up and licked the cigar. Then she lit the blunt, hitting it, passing it to me.

"Why you got them posted in the back of the car?"

"My album about to come out."

"Yea, how you going to put your album out and you beefing?" she said, hitting the blunt.

"Fuck them niggas."

"You know Slim killed Real last night, huh?"

"Yea, I heard that. That nigga got caught slipping."

"Baby, you got to be careful out chere."

"I got this." I stopped the car around the Melp project, hanging up posters. Then I pulled off heading to Canal Street. I got out hanging some posters at the bus stop. When I got back in my car, she was bumping my CD.

"Baby, this shit is hot."

"You feeling that?"

"You sound like Slim."

"Yea, I heard that before. But I'm better than that nigga."

"You are."

"Fuck him." I pulled up in the eight around St. Rock Park, hanging up posters.

***

Death

As I was sitting on the porch in the 8th ward smoking a blunt, talking to a couple of my niggas and selling dope, my fine ass bitch named Tina walked around the corner. Tina was a short bow-legged redbone with a fat ass and big titties, with freckles in her face, and blonde short hair. She had on gray gym shorts, halter top to match, and gray and black 1995 Air max I bought her.

She walked up and kissed me.

"Hey, baby."

"What's up, love?"

"That boy Soulja Slim around the park on St. Rock hanging up posters."

"What! You sure it's him?"

"I think so. Tall and brown-skinned with a lot of tattoos on him." I grabbed my gun off my lap and ran and jumped in my car.

I rode down fast looking for this nigga.

"I'm going to kill this fuck nigga. He got the nerve to come in my hood. I'm going to kill his ass!" I said, hitting on the steering wheel.

As I came around the park on St. Rock, I saw a nigga hanging up posters. This nigga going to disrespect me like this. I'm about to get some stripes off him.

I pulled up, slammed on the brake, and jumped out the car busting. I shot the nigga all in his back and head. I didn't give him a chance to run. The hoe in the car was screaming. I turned around and shot her twice in the face. Then I stood over him, finishing him. I jumped back in my car, pulling off.

"Momma, I got that nigga for you. I promised you I would and I did it. Love you, momma." I pulled back up on the set. I walked in the dope house where my girl and niggas was at counting and bagging up dope.

"You got him?" my niggas asked.

"You already know his ass is history."

***

Slim

"Damn! Mom, this fried chicken and red beans are good," I said, stuffing my mouth with the food.

"I'm glad you came to see me. After all this time."

"I'm sorry, busy trying to get this album finished."

"Yea. Well, you need to stick with that. All them nights I was crying, your ass was shot up in the hospital. You need to stay out them streets. Damn Magnolia projects! That place don't mean you no good."

"Yea, I hear you but I'm going to kill Murder."

"Your nephew—Jake?"

"Yes."

"What! Stop talking crazy."

"He the one that shot me up."

"What! Are you serious?"

"Yea, he took the hit on me."

"But he's your sister's kid."

"My step-sister on my daddy's side. His ass is dead."

"Slim, y'all need to talk about this."

"Mom, ain't shit to talk about. He chose his side. Now he got to pay."

"But—"

"Ain't no but. His ass is dead. Get your black dress."

"Damn! Y'all with this street shit."

"Get your black dress."

"But y'all family."

"His ass is dead." Just then the news came on and my mother's phone startedringing off the hook.

Today it was a bloody murder scene around St. Rock Park. A woman and man were shot several times in the head and body. People said he was Soulja Slim's nephew. And the bullets were meant for Soulja Slim. My mother walked back in the kitchen.

"That boy just got killed."

"I see it on the news."

"Hmm."

"Yea, fuck him. He had it coming anyway. From me. Somebody beat me to the punch."

"Slim, you shouldn't say that."

"I'm out, mom. Love you." I kissed her on the forehead."

"Be safe."

I walked out, getting in my truck, pulling off.

***

Joe

As Pepper and I was standing in the courtway serving bags, talking, Rena came around the corner with tears in her eyes and looking crazy.

"They just killed Murder in the 8th ward!"

"What the fuck!" I said.

"Are you sure?"

"Yes, it's on the news right now."

"Fuck!" I said. We ran in her apartment, seeing it for ourselves.

"Damn! Him and Poo."

"I wonder what he was doing down there," I said.

"Shit! He told me he was going to hang up some posters."

"Who was the nigga beefing with in the 8th ward?"

"Nobody that I know of," I said.

"Damn! You don't think Slim and Tre caught him, huh?"

"See, all this beef shit got my man killed. Get the fuck out my house!" Rena yelled.

"Murder know what it was," I said, walking to the door.

"You tripping," Pepper said.

"Yea, whatever. Y'all didn't even have his back!" said Rena.

"What the fuck ever!" I said.

"Nigga, let's go put this work in on them niggas."

"Let's do it." We walked to the hallway and grabbed the choppers. We walked through the cut on a mission, looking for Tre and Slim or whoever was out there.

"I feel you."

"Look, fuck whoever out. Them bitch going to feel what we feel."

"We going to let them have it."

"I'm with that."

***

Slim

When I pulled up in the project, Tre came walking up to my truck as I stepped out the truck.

"Man, you heard about that boy Murder, huh?"

"Yea, fuck him."

"Yea, they found his ass shot up in the eight ward."

"I heard. I don't feel shit for him. Fuck him."

"Slim, you got something?" Felicia said.

"Yea, let me go run inside." I walked in my apartment, grabbed the couple ounces of coke and dope. Along with the chopper and my .40 Glock. You never know a nigga might get to tripping back here.

I walked outside, sitting the chopper in the hallway. Then I went to serving coke and dope fiends.

I sat on the porch serving and talking to Craig and Tre.

Just then my phone rang. I looked at it and it was Big Sam out the Calliope. He was one of the big time drug dealers in the city. I used to take hits for the nigga.

"What's up, nigga?"

"I heard you was back. I was fucked up when they said you died."

"Na, you know they can't kill no soulja. What's up?"

"You feel like taking care of some business for me?"

"What it pay?"

"Ten thousand dollars"

"Okay, hit me up with the name."

"I got you later on."

"Cool."

As I hung up the phone, I saw some niggas coming through the cut with choppers in their hands. I drew my gun down as all hell broke loose. They went to hitting at us. I jumped in the hallway, and Craig and Tre ducked behind the dumper looking for shelter. People went to running and screaming, trying to get their kids out the way.

I hit back out the hallway with my chopper at Joe and Pepper. Tre and Craig busted back too. They exchanged fire a couple more seconds then they ran back through the cut.

I walked out the hallway looking up and down the courtway. Nobody was hurt. But I know the people was about to be back chere in a minute.

"Nigga, I'm out. I know the police about to rush in. Later." I dapped both them off, jumping in my truck, smashing out.

Chapter Ten

Slim

I pulled back into the projects around 12 o'clock. I sat on the steps in the dark Willow Courtway, dressed in all black, smoking on a hump with a .40 Glock on my lap. As I blew the smoke out my nose, thoughts of how I need to come up in this game crossed my mind. I'm tired of crumbling selling nickel- and-dime bags of heroin and coke in the projects. It's time to step my game up to the next level. I need to hook up with my cousin in Houston. Get my money right. Bond been on a nigga about putting this album out. I still need to pay for more studio time and I need some more money for the producer; this shit ain't cheap.

I don't give a fuck what's going on. I need that sticky in my life. And on top of that, nigga beefing, so that shit take always from a nigga hustle; a nigga got to be on full alert at all times.

This shit is crazy. You got to watch your back because your own people cut-throat you in the city of New Orleans. I see why they call this bitch *Cut-throat City*. If I decide to get a record label, that's what I'm going to call it: *Cut-throat Records*.

I hit the cigarette again, waiting on this nigga Sam to call me on this lick. I need this bitch too. My pockets hurting. All the money I have either go on drugs or studio time.

I clenched my gun when I saw a dope fiend walk toward me.

"Boy, I know you ain't grabbing no gun for me?" Anita said, walking toward me.

"What you want?"

"Give me two bags of dope."

"Man, you always want something!" I snapped.

"Boy, don't play with me. I use to change you for pampers."

I looked her up and down. She had on some cut-off blue jeans shorts, a white T-shirt and some brown sandals. Her hair was all over her head like she just finished turning a trick. I knew she probably did. Anita was one of the old dope fiends in the projects. She been drugging since I was a kid. She got a lot of kids: four boys, five girls. All her boys either in prison or dead. Her daughters—two were nurses, one a stripper and the other two were hoes on dope and fucking every balling nigga in the city.

My thoughts were interrupted by her begging me for some dope.

"Boy! Are you going to give it to me or not?" she said, scratching her red arms that had track marks on them from the dope needles.

"How much you got?" She rubbed her hand through her hair, smacking her lips and stared at me.

"Nothing."

"Man, look, this shit ain't free. Next time bring some money."

"Nigga, don't play with me 'cause your ass up." I was just fucking with her. I was going to give it to her. Anita was the first piece of pussy I got. I fucked her and her other big fine friend— Steph. She loved that dope.

I stood up whispering for Len. She came to the window and looked out.

"What's good?" she said.

"Drop two packs of heroin out the window."

"A'ight." Len dropped the two silver foil packs out the window. Anita walked over and picked them up.

"Preciate you son," she said, walking off fast, not evening looking back.

She called everybody nigga in the hood 'son' because she probably raised you at her house. She used to run a daycare spot in the project.

I sat back on the steps, and fired up a blunt. As I was hitting it, my phone rang. I pulled it off my hip and looked at the number. It was the call I was waiting on.

"Woo Na, Sam."

"What's up, Slim?

"You ready?"

"Yea, look, I need you to handle some business for me."

"I'm on the way." I stood up put the gun in my waist and hollered for Len.

"Yea."

"Shut it down. I got to go handle some business."

"You coming back tonight?"

"I don't know."

"Okay. Be careful." As I jumped in my truck, my phone rang. It was this bitch named Trina out the east I had met a couple weeks ago.

"What's up?" I said.

"You coming through tonight."

"Yea, I got to handle something but I'm coming through."

"Okay." I pulled out the projects, heading up Washington Ave., and turned on Claiborne. As I turned on MLK headed to the Calliope, I went thinking back how I first met Sam. It was through my brother. He put me down and I took my first hit and he paid me 10,000 grand to kill this big time drug dealer out the Florida named Whitey.

And we been rocking since. I know he would put a nigga down, but I have to kill Sam if I fuck his shit up. Plus his price on keys are high; he want $90,000 a brick. I can get it cheap and not step on from my cousin. But I don't want to go broke. So I'm going to try and get about $50,000 up then holla at him.

I turned off MLK and parked my car in front of this reddish brick bar room called Rose's Tavern across the street from the reddish brick Calliope projects. I stepped out the car with my gun under my arm, as I looked around. As I walked toward the bar room, I looked at the wall that had a lot of rest- in-peace names on it written in black and red writing with their names.

Better them than me, I thought to myself, walking into the bar.

I looked around for Sam and spotted him sitting at the table in the corner. He had a few niggas around him with guns dressed in all-black suit.

He had on some black slack, a white long-sleeved shirt and some black Stacy Adams shoes. Sam was big, dark-skinned with a bald head and snow-white beard.

He ran a lot drugs in the city. He was an old player from way back. He had a lot of respect in the city, because he did ten years in the feds and never ratted on no one. He came home and got on and blew up. Now he got some of uptown lock with heroin. And he be quick to put a hit on a nigga head about playing with his money. Or to get rid of the competition in the city.

Before I sat down, his bodyguard patted me down and took my gun.

I sat down at the table across from him as he put his cigar out in the ashtray.

"What's up, Sam?"

"I need you to handle some business for me."

"Who is it?"

"This nigga Roc from downtown. He been owing me forty grand for about a month now and he call hisself ducking me. I need you to make this nigga ass make the news."

"Okay."

"Here the ten grand." He slid the envelope. I picked it up, walking out.

I got back in the truck, pulling off, thinking to myself where can I catch this nigga slipping at. He liked to hang around clubs. He liked to stunt for the hoes. I thought about what today was; it was Friday night. The daiquiri shop be jumping. I took a ride around there to see if I could see him. He wasn't there. Then I rode around the detour that was down the street from the Melp project. I spotted his car in the middle of the street. He was flossing in his blue 500 Benz talking to some hoes.

I jumped out my truck with a chopper, creeping between cars, making sure the nigga don't see me. When he looked up, I had the chopper hit at him.

Roc's brain splattered all over the car and them hoes and me. The crowd started screaming. I blended in with them as I ran back to my car, pulling off.

I dialed Sam's number.

"Yea."

"It's done." *Click.* I pulled back in the Magnolia, went inside, and put my chopper in the closet. I jumped in the shower, allowing the hot water to rinse the blood off me. As I stepped out the shower drying off, I heard my phone ring. I walked in the room and picked it up. It was Trina.

"Woo, what's up, love?"

"I thought you was coming through."

"I'm on the way."

"Okay."

I looked at the clock; it read: 1 o'clock. I threw on a white polo shirt with some blue Girbaud's and my Reeboks, with my *Saint* hat turned to the back.

I grabbed some money, my gun and keys, and headed out the door.

I drove to her house that was located in the Eastern part of New Orleans. It's a big coke, dope and weed set. Niggas been getting killed around here for years. Plus it be super dark around here. I stepped out my truck with the .40 in my hand walking through the gate in a dark courtway going to her house.

She was waiting for me with her hands on her hips, barefoot with her hair wrapped in a pink bandanna and see- through teddy on with her brown nipples hard. She was young, around nineteen years old, caramel-skinned, 5'3 and wide-hipped. She had hazel eyes and a round fat ass. I had met her a couple weeks ago at Lakeside Mall when I was shopping for some gear. She had on some tight blue jeans, a pink Bebe shirt and some white Reeboks.

She was with her friend at Foot Locker, checking out some tennis. So I stepped up to her and asked her name. I brought the Air Max she was looking at. Then I got her number.

Weeks went by. I forgot all about her with all the beefing shit I had going on. Until she hit me up a few weeks ago asking me to come over.

"Damn! About time you come and fuck with a bitch?" she said with an attitude

"I been busy."

"Whatever. Come in."

"You don't have nigga living here, huh?"

"No, I don't play them games."

"Just checking. You know these chicks in New Orleans."

"I'm not like them."

"I hear you. You got some to smoke?" I walked over, sitting on her couch in front the big floor model TV.

She walked back with the blunt in her hand, passing it to me. We smoked and chilled for seconds. As I laid back on the couch, she went to massaging my dick, getting it hard. I didn't say a word. I let her do her. She unzipped my jeans, putting my dick out. She leaned over, deep-throating it and sucking on my balls. She climbed on top of me, riding my dick, as I bounced her up and down, grabbing her ass cheeks as she bit my shoulder, shaking.

"Fuck! Boy, I'm coming," she said, shaking all the way.

We moved to her bedroom where I spread her ass cheeks and went to hitting her from the back. I pulled her as I slammed my dick deeper into her pussy wall, causing her to shiver and come again. She gripped the bed sheet, slamming her ass back on my dick.

"I'm coming again." I flipped her over and put her in the buck with her toes touching the head board as I thrusted in and out of her pussy.

"Fuck! About to come again," she said, pulling me to her.

"Me too." We came together. She came all over my dick and I shot all my hot nut in her. We lay there catching our breath.

"Damn! Nigga, you got some good dick."

"Your pussy fire too. I don't see why you ain't got no older man."

"I did. He got killed in the uptown, in the Calliope a couple months ago."

"Oh." That dope still had my dick hard. She climbed back on top and rode my dick all night.

Chapter Eleven

Slim

I sat on the porch in the Magnolia the next evening with a .357, waiting on Tre to pull up. Niggas in my project give me a couple ounces to make some money.

But that wasn't shit. I shot a couple grams in my arm a day. Yea, nigga back getting loaded. Fuck it. This how I'm rocking.

Just then my phone rang.

"Whoa, nigga, what up?" I asked.

"Nigga, they said they not fucking with you like that there."

"So a nigga drop from the label for real. Damn! Fuck them hoes. Back to the grind. I gotta come up with some money to get this album."

"Okay, I'm trying to work on some show for you."

"A'ight, later, my nigga."

"Later." Tre walked up to dapping me off.

"What up, nigga?"

"Shit, this nigga Bond just called me and said the label dropped me.

"Damn! That fuck up."

"It's cool. I'ma use hustling to get my own shit."

"Who you had a shoot-out with the other night?"

"This nigga Joe who run with my nephew."

"Oh, but look—I got a lick for some money."

"Who?"

"Nigga Derk out the 17th. He keep a lot of money in his house."

"Okay, because I can get us plugged in with my cousin on some dope. He playing with a couple keys of heroin."

"Cool. Nigga, let's pull off this act first."

"Let's roll. We pulled up to this nice house in Slidell on the outskirt of New Orleans.

It had a big Bentley parked in the driveway.

"Damn! The nigga not here."

"What kind of car the nigga drive?"

"A 500 SL Benz—black."

"Okay, we chill till this nigga come home," I said, passing the blunt.

We sat there for about an hour waiting on this nigga to come. I was getting restless and ready to go. Thinking to myself: *I'll catch this nigga later on.* As I was about to pull off, I saw the nigga's car pull in the driveway. I was parked a couple houses down. He stepped out of the car with a fine yellow bone with blonde hair.

"Nigga, you ready?" I asked him.

"Let's do it." We jumped out of the car, running up to him as they made their way to the door.

"Nigga, don't move!" I said, putting the gun in his back.

"Bitch, you better not scream or I'm going to kill right here." We pushed them inside the house. Derk was tall, slim, black with a low haircut and waves.

"Where the money?" I asked.

"Nigga, fuck you! I ain't giving you shit."

"Okay, nigga, this how you want to play this?" We tied them both up.

"Please let me go. I won't tell on you!" she cried.

I put the gun to the bitch's head.

"Nigga, get us the money or I'm going to blow this bitch's head off."

"Derk, give them the money."

"Fuck that bitch nigga."

I shot her in the head.

"Nigga, you next."

"Man, fuck y'all. I'm not scared to die!" Tre shot him in the head twice.

"I got tired of the nigga talking shit."

"Let's search the house." We went through each room, tearing it up.

We went to the master bedroom where we searched good and found money in the clothes safe.

They had a stack of wrapper bands on it. We stuffed them in a pillow case.

We took money, jewelry and a few choppers. We ran out the house, got in the truck and smashed out. As we sat in Len's house counting the money, it came up to $100,000.

"Dope," I said.

"Man, look, I can get cuz to get us a cheap price on some."

"Nigga, hook that up."

"I'm going to holla at him tomorrow."

"Bet."

Robert Baptiste

Chapter Twelve

Slim

We pulled up at my cousin's house on the Southside of Houston. He has a small white brick mansion in Sugar Land. They had a bunch of people there; it looked like he had a party going on.

When we walked up to the door, a couple bodyguards tried to stop us from coming in the house."

"Who are you?" they asked us.

"Man, this my cousin shit."

"We don't know you."

"Man, call Luke before I shoot yo' ass in the face," I said.

As Tre and I was about to pull our guns, Luke walked up to the door.

"Whoa, hold up. Slim, y'all put the guns away."

"Man, these niggas was trying—"

"It's cool. Come on in. Let's have some fun. Man, we got plenty drugs and bitches."

"Luke, this my nigga Tre."

"Nice to meet you."

"This our money." He took the bag and handed it to the bodyguard.

"Hold up, cousin. It's eighty K in the bag."

"Don't worry about it. Come, let's go have fun, cousin . You and your friend. We handle business in the morning."

"Cool," I said.

They had a lot of bitches everywhere in thongs with no tops on; some were butt-naked in the pool. All shapes and sizes, different nationalities.

He had a couple hoes walking around with plates of drugs— pills, coke, weed and heroin.

Just then a white girl stopped in front of us with all different color pills on a tray.

"X-pills. You never try them?"

"Na."

"You don't know what you missing. This shit keep your dick hard like heroin."

"Okay. Let me try then."

"Me too." We both popped some blue dolphins; that's what they are called.

"Okay, now let's party." Next thing you know, them bitch had our jaws tight and we fell like we was rolling. They had us horny as shit.

For the rest of the night we fucked bitches by the two's.

I woke up with my mouth dry as a motherfucker. I got up, walked in the bathroom sipping water out the sink and splashing it on my face.

"Damn! Them had a nigga right. And fucking good. I need to fuck with them some more." I walked back in the room looking at the white girl butt-naked laying in the bed. I got dressed and walked around the house looking for Tre.

When I walked downstairs, he was talking to my cousin in the living room

"I'm glad you could join us, cousin."

"Nigga, about time you got up. Wild night, huh?"

"Nigga, truthfully, I don't remember none of it."

"Well, sit down, cousin. You hurry."

"No, I need to kill this morning sickness."

He slapped his hand and a slim Indian looking chick with long black hair came in. She brought a plate of dope and sat on the table.

I hit a line of it to kill my sickness. Tre did the same.

"What you looking to buy?"

"A key. Damn! This shit good," I said.

"Yea, this is fire!" Tre said.

"Okay. Normally, my keys go for a hundred and twenty thousand dollars. But since you my cousin, I'm going to give it to for eighty thousand. I'll front you some keys. I'll give you two keys. Bring my hundred and twenty thousand back on from there."

"Sound good to me."

"Okay." He clapped his hand and the same woman came out with a briefcase and placed it on the table. I opened it up, and it was keys uncut.

"Pure China white. Never been stepped on."

"Cool. Cousin, we out!" I said, dapping him off.

"Look, take this bag of pills with you. Sell them. It's the next drug."

"How many in the bag?"

"That's a thousand. Holla at me, tell me what it do. The hoes going to love making them freak."

"Okay. Cool. Later."

***

Slim

The next evening Tre, Len and I sat in her kitchen breaking down the brick of heroin. My cousin said it could take a seven. That mean in the dope world you can make seven keys off one. And the shit still be good.

But I'm going to drop five on this shit and make some testers and see what the dope fiends have to say.

"Nigga, I'm trying to have this bitch on fire like them niggas in the St. Thomas did with the 911."

"For sure."

"Len, get the mannitol." We sat in there for hours on end. Bagging up and breaking down. We cut up foil papers, dropping big line in each one of them.

"We going to sell our bags for twenty dollars."

"I'm with that."

"And guess what?"

"What that?"

"We going to have the city on lock."

"I feel you."

"So off ounces we going to make like twelve bands."

"I dig that." We finished bagging up everything around twelve at night. We walked outside in the circle looking for dope fiends. We handed out sample bags to a lot of them. I saw this old dope fiend named Fish.

"Fish, try this shit. It some new shit. Tell what you think."

"Okay."

Then I handed out a few more.

The next morning I came out of Len's house about five in the morning, because that's when dope fiends looking to get that morning fix and the rush coming.

It was a welfare line up waiting on me. It was like I was handing out government cheese.

"Slim, that shit you gave Fish was fire. He OD'd last night," Reena said. "I'm trying to get some of that shit." *Damn! That nigga die last night*, I thought to myself.

Shit! That dope is good.

See, in the heroin game when a nigga die off your shit, that's a good thing; that mean the dope is good.

As soon as dope fiends hear that, it's going to be on; every dope fiends, niggas and hoes going to come cop from us.

The best thing about the dope was that a dope fiend could snort or shoot it.

Before I went to serving, I snorted a bag to get the monkey of me. As I was serving, Tre walked up.

"Man, what's good."

"Nigga OD'd last night on the dope."

"That what up."

"Look, we going to sell bags until we make our money back."

"I'm with that." We served for a couple hours straight making money hand over feet.

Chapter Thirteen

Slim

Trina and I drove back from my cousin's house with two bricks of dope. I paid him the money we owed him. We got our own block apiece.

He gave me two bags of pills. He told me to bring him four grand back. Them motherfuckaz move faster than the dope. I might sell a whole thousand of pills in two weeks. I was selling them ten dollars a pill.

Them X pills had New Orleans on fire.

Them double stack blue dolphins and yellow pills had them hoes freaked out their mind. Them hoes was willing to do anything for it. Them niggas in the city was on them and killing everything moving.

I looked over at Trina; she was rolling on them pills.

Trina and I got real close in the last couple months.

She began moving pills on Taraline for me in the East and holding my guns and dope over there.

I even been moving dope around there, giving them nigga quarters and grams.

"Slim, my pussy on fire," she said, rubbing on my dick.

"Shit, what you want me to do?"

She undid my pants, stroking my dick.

"Girl, you tripping."

"Just keep your eyes on the road." She went down, deep-throating my dick.

"Fuck, girl! You almost made me crash."

She rose up and climbed on top of my dick, riding my dick.

She rode my dick until she came. She got off me and went to playing with her pussy, coming and shaking all over my seat.

"Shit, them pills got me on fucking fire."

We pulled up to her house. I grabbed the black bag and brought it into her house. I stashed a brick and 500 pills in her A/C vent. I had 100,000 over here.

"Baby, give me some dick before you leave. My pussy on fire."
I bent her over the sofa, slamming my dick in her from the back as she pushed back on me. Her pussy was soaking wet.

"Fuck! Baby, don't stop. I'm coming." She shook so hard like she was about to have a seizure. I shot hot come all in her. I pulled up my pants and grabbed my gun and bag, about to head out the door.

"Baby, where you going? I'm still horny as shit."

"Shit, I got to handle business. Go get a dildo and get off. I'm out."

"Fuck, Slim! I need some dick."

"You should pop them pills. I'm out."

***

Slim

I sat at the table in my apartment in the project, counting money and bagging up silver foil packs with Craig, Tre, and Len. I gave Tre his brick already.

"Nigga, my cousin fronted us two of them things. It's on now! I told you, nigga, we was going to get this this money fucking with my cousin."

"Nigga, how much we got?"

"Two hundred and fifty thousand," Craig said, hitting the blunt.

"Okay. We need to be sending my cousin his money. We owe him a hundred and eighty thousand for the pills and the two bricks."

"I'm on it," Tre said.

I put Craig on the team because that's Tre's man and he's a good nigga.

"Man, I got to go make a couple moves."

"Look, let me holla at you," Tre said, walking outside with me.
"What's good?"

"Nigga, word on the street them *8th ward Animal* nigga trying to kill you."

"What!"

"Yea, when they kill your nephew it was meant for you."

"What the fuck! What that shit about?"

"Shit, that back-in-the-day shit when we went in that house."

"Nigga, I told you we should have killed all them motherfuckaz."

"I know, just watch your back."

"Later."

I jumped in my truck, smashing out. I had to make a couple stops in the French Quarter I was serving a couple white people.

I pulled up to this old white house in the quarter that had a black gate on it. I stepped out with two ounces in my hand. I walked to the gate and knocked on the door.

Shelly came to the door wearing some cut-off jeans and white t-shirt.

Shelly and her husband work in the French quarter at Bars.

"Come in, Slim." I walked in. Chad was sitting down fixing the dope in the spoon. He was a slim white guy with sandy blond hair.

"What's up, Slim?"

"Nothing. Here, the quarters." Shelly handed me the 3000 grand.

"Thanks, Slim," she said,

"You want to hit some?" Chad asked.

"Na, I'm good. I'm out."

I made a couple more moves uptown serving niggas grams and quarters. Then I pulled back up on Taraline. I jumped with my pistol in my hand. Dope fiends and niggas and hoes was trying to cop some dope. It was like a welfare line out there. I was serving while Trina collected the money. The rush lasted a good thirty minutes. After it slowed down, I went inside counting the money. I made ten grand right fast.

As we were bagging up some more dope, somebody knocked at the door.

"Who is it?" Trina said.

"Me, Treasure." Trina opened the door, letting her in. Treasure was a fine yellow thick bone that I want to fuck. She gave her number a couple time but a nigga be moving fast.

"What's up, Slim?"

"Coolin."

"What you trying to get?" Trina asked.

"Two blue pills."

"You trying to get fuck good, huh?"

"You already know it."

"Here." She handed Trina forty dollars and smiled at me.

"Later, Slim."

"Later."

"That hoe want to fuck you?"

"Yea."

"I can tell how she look at you."

"Well, you need to see if she down to have a threesome."

"I don't want you to fuck that nasty asshole with your dick. That bitch fuck everybody on the line."

"Well, I'm about to go. I need to drop some of this money off at my house."

"Okay, holla at me."

I grabbed the money. It was $250,000 in the bag. I walked out the house, getting in my truck, pulling off.

I made it to my girl's house. She was gone. I walked in the room putting the money in the safe. I laid across the bed tired as shit, falling asleep.

Chapter Fourteen

Flav

I rode around uptown looking for these niggas Slim and Tre. Them motherfuckaz ran into my brother's house and killed him. I promised my brother Derk at his funeral that I was going to kill these niggas, and that's what I'm going to do.

As we rode down Louisiana Ave., headed toward the Magnolia, I spotted them niggas hanging and chilling, leaning on Slim's truck. They were talking to some hoes and niggas

"There them nigga is right there," Dice said.

"I see, turn around." As he turned around, I cocked the chopper and rolled down my window. As soon as he pulled up, I went to hitting at them. Slim and Tre went to running along with the crowd of people. I busted at them going through the cut in the project. I hit one nigga in the back and in the head. And hit a girl in the leg.

"Nigga pulled off. Fuck! I miss them niggas." We pulled back in the 17th ward in Gert Town, getting out on the set.

"You got them nigga?" Dice asked.

"No. I miss them nigga."

"Fuck!" Dice was my little brother. He be hanging with my nigga in front this bar on the corner where we be pumping dope and shooting dice. My brother Derk had this bitch sold up. But now I took it over.

"I'm going to get them niggas if it's the last thing I do."

"Next time I'm coming with you."

"I hear you," I said, sitting on the drain, smoking weed, watching niggas sell my heroin to people.

***

Slim

Tre and I ran back in the projects ducking the chopper bullets. I know it wasn't Joe and Pepper; them niggas were in jail on some murders out the 8th ward. They killed some nigga on music. They back town fighting them charges.

"Nigga, you know who that was?" I said, breathing hard.

"Yea, that was that nigga Flav out the 17th."

"Who?"

"Derk brother. The nigga we killed."

"Yea, I forgot all about that nigga." Just then Skiddlez high yellow ass with all the tattoos over her body with pink hair came up the courtway.

"Y'all know Lil' Billy got killed, huh?"

"What!"

"Damn!" I said.

"And Lemon got shot in the legs. The police around there now." Tre and I walked on the other side of the projects. We watched as Billy's mother cry over his body.

Lil' Billy was about no trouble; all he did was hustle a little weed in the project and went to school and fuck a couple young bitches in the projects. They put Lemon ass in the back of the ambulance and pulled off. They covered Billy up in the white sheet, putting his body on the stretcher and put it in the other ambulance, pulling off.

"Nigga, we got to ride for Lil' Billy," Tre said.

"You already know."

***

The whole Magnolia was outside at the park and on Washington, watching the second line go by with Lil' Billy's casket. They had the second line band and people second line for him. I paid for everything and even gave his mother some money. He did have nothing to do with the beef we had going on. I felt sorry for him, and Lemon chocolate ass was out of the hospital on crushes.

"Damn! My nigga, I really feel bad for his mother," I said.

"What you want to do?"

"Let's ride on these niggas." Tre, Craig and I jumped in my truck with fully load chopper with bandana clips on them, headed to the 17th ward, trying to catch these niggas slipping.

We spun the corner by the Blue Plate Factory. I spotted them niggas setting on the drain hustling dope. I jumped out with my chopper along with Tre, busting shots. They went to running. Craig jumped out busting shots. Niggas came out of a few dope houses hitting with 9mm.

We were in a shoot-out for a couple minutes until the police went to hitting the block. We jumped in, smashing out.

"Damn! We ain't get them niggas," I said.

"We going to spin on their ass again. This shit not over with."

"For sure," Craig said. We pulled up in the project going into the courtway. I got the dope and went to pumping it as we sat on the porch smoking weed, shooting dope and chilling.

Robert Baptiste

Chapter Fifteen

Slim

A couple months later, we had the 'nolia on fire. The circle was off the chain. DJs every day, money flowing through the project, niggas and hoes coming from all over to chill and score dope and pills or just to hang out. The Magnolia was the place to be in '97.

As I was sitting on the steps smoking on a blunt, Tricky walked up to me.

Tricky was a young nigga who went to juv' for robbing a bank. Him and a couple more bad motherfuckaz in the projects.

"What's good, Slim?"

"Coolin."

"Man, put me down on some dope. So I can get some money. You know a nigga fresh home."

"I got you. Holla at me a little bit later. But here's five hundred dollars."

"Good looking out, Slim." I don't have a problem with showing the hood love. Tre and I was putting a lot of niggas on when they got out. I had the project on lock with the dope my cousin was sending me. I even had a couple nigga on the Taraline pushing dope and pills for me; they was giving the money to Trina for me.

Just then my phone rang. It was DJ Mike. He told me to come on the Parkway to his studio; he had some beat for my new album.

"Nigga, y'all hold it down. I gotta go holla at Mike," I said, dapping them off.

"Later, Slim, you be cool." I pulled up to DJ Mike's house on the Parkway. It was a green and white house that was made out of wood. He had a studio in there.

I walked up to the house, knocking on the door. I could hear the beat bumping outside. He came to the door, letting me in. I followed him upstairs to the room where he had the studio equipment and sound booth. I walked in nodding to the beat.

"You like that, huh?"

"Fucking right." I sat down rolling up a blunt, listening to the beat. Rapping a rap in my head for it.

"Man, give me a pad." I went to smoking and writing the rap down on the paper. I blew the smoke out my mouth and nose as I nodded to the beat.

"Let's do it." I walked in the booth laying the rap down to the beat. I did it in one take. I walked out as he was smiling nodding.

"You like that there, huh?"

"Man, I like that motherfucker."

"You got another beat?"

"Yea, you know I stay loaded." He put on another beat. That bitch went hard than the first one. I rolled another blunt up, grabbing the pad, writing another rap to the beat, smoking.

I went back in, laying this rap down called *Make it Happen*.

"Nigga, you did that shit."

"You like that shit, huh?"

"That bitch on point."

"This album here. Going to be like that."

"So who you going to put this album out under?"

"I was thinking about doing some independent."

"Man, I know somebody at No Limit."

"I'm good."

"Man, look, it can give you a chance to get in other states." Fuck this local shit."

"I don't know."

"Look—"

"Man, I can see all my money right chere," I said, blowing the smoke out my nose."

"Well, you can make your own contract. It's better than sitting around motherfuckers selling dope. Try to get the hood with this shit. At least let's see where it can take you."

"Okay, fuck, let's see what it can do."

"Okay, I'm going to holla at Rob, the nigga that run that shit."

"Let that nigga know he fuck with that money—his ass going to die."

"I got this."

"A'ight, let's finish laying down some tracks."

***

Slim

I pulled up to this white tall brick building with a glass door and windows with *No Limit* written in black and red ink. Mike, Bond and I stepped out of my truck. I had on some dark blue Girbaud's, a white wife-beater with a throwback Saints jersey on, with the Saint's cap turned to the back, and my black Soulja Reeboks.

When we walked in, I looked around at all the platinum and gold albums on the wall. Mike walked up to the desk letting the secretary know we were here for our appointment.

We sat on the black leather sofa in the front. I looked at all the local rappers from the city that was on their label. They were either gold or platinum.

Ten minutes later, a tall black guy came out wearing a black suit and black Gator with a fade and waves in them.

"What's up, Rob?" Mike said, shaking his hand.

"Nothing, it's all good."

"How you, Soulja Slim?"

"I'm coolin," I said, not shaking his hand.

"Come on, follow me." We followed him into the elevator all the way to the 10th floor, then we followed him into a conference room that had a big brown table and black leather chair.

"Y'all have a seat."

"Let's get down to business. I got somewhere to be," I said.

"Okay, look, Slim, we want you to come to *No Limit*. We can get your stuff nationwide. I just signed a deal with Priority Record so now I'm nationwide. And I think you'll be a great fix."

"What we talking?"

"I'm going to sign you to a two album deal. I'm going to give you a quarter million, a Rolex watch and a Tank chain.

"Okay, look, I got a few raps I did already."

"Cool, put them on the album."

"Okay. You get a deal." We shook hands.

I signed the contract.

"Now let's make this money. Welcome to the tank."

***

Slim

Three Weeks Later

I pulled up to the studio in Metairie that Master P had bought for the local rapper to come and use to lay their music down.

It was a brown and glass building with all new shit inside. When I walked in the studio, Bond was in there with a new producer that was making tracks. They were listening to the beats.

'What's Wootay?" I said, dapping both of them off.

'Coolin," Bond said. "You need to get on some of these fire beats."

"That's what I came to do. You feel me." I sat down listening to a couple of them beat, smoking a blunt and writing a rap down on paper.

As I was bopping my head to this one track, the words to this rap went to falling on the paper.

"I got it."

"Let me hear it," Bond said.

"This the hook, Boss man."

"Go in the booth and spit it." I went in the booth, spit the rap in one take.

I watched as they bobbed their heads.

I walked out dapping them off.

"Y'all like that, huh?" I said, hitting the blunt.

"Fucking right." I went back in the booth to lay a few more songs down.

Then I sat back and listened to a few beats."

"You got a name for the album?"

"Yea—*Give it 2 'em Raw*."

"I like that."

"You dig."

"Man, don't blow this lick."

"I'm trying not to."

"Damn! Slim. You getting shot ain't change shit."

"Fuck no. I'm going to be who I am until I'm dead. And I'm going to kill the bitch that shot me up. Man, the fucking streets— That's who made me—The streets." I hit the blunt and listened to the track I just put down.

Robert Baptiste

Chapter Sixteen

Slim

1998 Album Release Party

I pulled up in front of this club in New Orleans East called *Whisper*. It was one of the popping clubs in the city.

I parked my gray new Montero Sport that was sitting on 26-inches chrome rims and tinted windows. I was blasting my new CD that was about to drop sometime in July. I was bumping my song *Wootay* that was the hot single on the streets. Then I had another single they were playing in the club. From what I was told, them hoes and niggas go crazy in the club when it come on.

Cash Money was on too. They had a few niggas from out my projects that were on their label, and few niggas from uptown too making some noise like the little nigga I fuck with out the 13th ward named BG. Him and Juv was holding it down for that uptown.

I stepped out with my new shit I was bringing to the city. I was camouflaged down with the army boots, rag on my head and the hat to match. Plus I had the .40 on my hip in case a nigga was trying to get fucked up tonight.

This promotional party was going to help my album sales.

I walked in the club full of dope and heroin. The DJ was playing my song, *Wootay*.

Tre and the whole uptown and the Magnolia project was in here.

I jumped on the stage as the DJ dropped the beat. The whole place went crazy, rapping the whole song. Then I performed a couple old songs.

I stepped off the stage sweating like a motherfucka. They give me daps and hugs. I went in the bathroom, snorted a line of dope and popped a couple pills. As I came out the bathroom, this bitch— Treasure—walked up to me rolling on some pills. She had on some tight green knickerbockers with a pink tight Bebe shirt and pink Bebe heels. Her hair was long in a ponytail.

"What's up, Slim?" She smiled.

"Coolin. What you got going on?"
"Shit, I'm trying to see what's good."
"Shit, it all good with me."
"Well, me and girlfriend trying to go to the hotel tonight."
"I'm fucking down."
"Okay, let's go," she said.
I went to dapp Tre off and few other niggas out the project.

***

Trina

As soon as Slim left to go to the party that I didn't feel like going to, I went in the room, pulling out the silver bullet because them pills had a bitch pussy on fire. I need to come bad. That nigga should stay and give me that dick.

As I was in the room getting off and coming like a motherfucker, somebody knocked at the door. I wasn't going to stop, but I need to get up and make this money.

I walked to the door, looked through the peephole; it was Simfany fine ass. She was light brown-skinned, thick with long dreads and a pretty face, and I heard she on pussy. I might get this bitch to eat me out.

"What's up, Simfany?"
"I need a couple of pills. Bitch, it smell like weed in here."
"You trying to blow something?"
"Always." I walked back in the living room with a blunt and pills in my hand.

"Here," I watched as she popped the pills, hit the weed and passed it back to me.

"Damn! This shit good," she said, choking, passing it back to me.

We sat there for a while blowing.

Next thing—we looked at each other with lust in our eyes.

"What's up?" I smiled.

"Whatever." She played in her hair.

94

We went to the back room, getting naked. We got in the bed and started eating each other out.

We were in the 69, coming back to back in each other's mouth. Then we got into a scissors position, rubbing our pussy together. As we were about to come, I heard the front door come flying open.

Some niggas with guns and masks on their face rushed in my room pointing their guns. One of the niggas grabbed me by the hair, pulling me out the bed and the other nigga did her the same.

"Bitch, where the money and drugs?" he said, pointing the gun in my face.

I was crying and shaking. So was Simfany.

"In the A/C vent," I said. They tied us up with the phone cords and put duct tape over our mouth.

Then I heard them going in the vent.

"Nigga, this is a hella of lick." I recognized the nigga voice. It was a nigga named Flame .

"You fucking right."

"And see them nigga hang together. Wait until I tell Slim. He going to kill their ass.

***

Slim

My cell phone beeped and was ringing off the chain. That's the shit that woke me up. I looked at it and it was Trina with 911 behind everything. Damn, this was wild as fuck last night. Them pills had them niggas doing everything and taking it in all their holes. I looked at the two fine bitches in the bed. This bitch Treasure is a beast; her and her friend. I don't even know the bitch's name. We fucked and drugged all night popping pills, snorting dope and drinking. We had a ball for real.

My phone rang again. It was Trina.

I hope ain't nothing happened. Because I left her house, and she was mad as fuck because I don't want to stay and fuck her.

"Woo Na. What's good?"

"Nigga, where you at! I been calling your ass all night."

"Hold the fuck up, you don't call here checking me about shit. You the bitch, I'm the nigga. Now what up?"

"Nigga ran in this motherfucker last night, tied me up and robbed me."

"What the fuck! I'm on my way." I grabbed my pants, threw them on with the rest of my clothes. I grabbed my gun, running out the hotel and jumped in my truck.

I pulled up on Taraline, slamming on the brakes, jumping out with my gun in my hand, running up to Trina's apartment. When I walked in, I looked around; shit was trashed: sofa, TV. Everything was everywhere, and she was pacing back and forward.

"What happened?"

"Two niggas ran in here, tied me up and put the gun in my head and made me tell them where the money and drugs were at."

"Fuck!" I walked over to the A/C vent, looked in there and everything was gone. "Fuck! Did you get a voice?"

"Yea."

"Who was it?"

"Flame and Dee."

"I'm going to kill them motherfucker."

I walked outside to see if I seen them niggas around. They wasn't out.

"Fuck! Look, if you see them nigga, call me."

"Okay."

"I'm going to be back."

"Okay."

"Here, a stack."

"Call me."

"I got you."

I jumped in my truck, pulling off mad as fuck. I rode around the city with my head fucked up. I was thinking about where I could catch these bitch ass niggas. I thought about Trina, thinking whether she let them niggas in her apartment. But that hoe know not to play with me. I blew the smoke out my mouth and nose. I pulled up in the project, and Tre jumped in my truck.

"Nigga, what's good?"

"Man, niggas went in my little bitch house in the east and took my shit."

"Who? Trina?"

"Yea."

"What they took?"

"Quarter mil. A key of dope."

"Damn! Nigga. We need to find them niggas."

"You fucking right."

"You sure that bitch ain't had nothing to do with it?"

"Man, that bitch wouldn't play with me like that."

"Nigga, you know you can't trust these hoes out chere in the city. This shit is cut-throat out chere. Her ass gone too funny."

"I feel you. If I find out that bitch had something to do with it, I'ma snuff her out."

"For sure. How much you got left?"

"A quarter million."

"I got about a hundred and fifty. Between snort dope and tricking. Money."

"I feel you."

"I'ma fuck with you later."

"Later."

Robert Baptiste

Chapter Seventeen

Slim

A month went by. I still haven't seen them niggas. I been through Taraline a couple time but I still never seen them niggas. I had put $25,000 on them niggas' heads.

As I was sitting in the project counting this money, my phone rang. It was Trina.

"What's up, love?"

"These niggas around here right now."

"A'ight, I'm on my way."

"What's good?" Tre asked.

"Shit, I'm gonna kill these niggas."

"Okay, let's handle this shit."

"Craig, you and Len make sure the money straight."

"Okay." We jumped in the truck, pulling off.

I made it to Taraline less than thirty minutes.

I was talking to Trina the whole way, making sure they were still out there.

When I spun the corner, I saw them niggas.

I jumped out the truck, running up to the nigga Flame, busting him up before he could pull his gun. Tre shot Dee in the face.

I shot Flame fifteen times, emptying the clip on him.

I grabbed Tre's gun, finishing the other nigga off.

We jumped back in the truck, pulling off.

I dropped Tre off in the project.

"Good looking out," I said.

"For sure."

***

Slim

When I walked in the house, Kim stood there looking at me.

"Slim, why you got the blood on you?"

"I just killed two niggas."

"What! What for?"

"They took a key of heroin and quarter million from a friend of mine. The dope and money was mine," I said, as I walked to the bedroom with her on my heels. I put away the gun.

"Look, take these clothes and get rid of them."

"Okay."

I went and jumped in a hot shower, letting water rinse the blood off. A couple minutes later, Kim joined me. We went to kissing each other. I picked her up, sliding my dick in her, bouncing her up and down on my hardness.

"Fuck! Yes, Slim. I love you!" she said, coming.

I carried her to the bedroom, laying her on the bed, going down on her. I ate her pussy out as she grabbed my head, shaking and coming all on my mouth. I put her legs on my shoulders, thrusting in and out of her as we came together.

She laid her head on my chest, dozing off to sleep. As I was dozing, I heard the front door bust open. I went to grab my gun and bust two holes in the bedroom door. My girl jumped on the floor.

"This is the fucking police."

"How do I know that?"

"Because this N.O.P.D"

"Y'all could be pretending." See, back in the day niggas was faking dressed up like the police robbing and killing niggas. The white boy threw the police badges on the floor.

"N.O.P.D!"

They pushed me to the bed, hand-cuffing me. They allowed my girl to put on some clothes.

"Man, what did I do?"

"We talk to you at the station."

"I need some clothes." They helped me out with some jeans, slippers and T-shirts.

"What did he do?" she screamed at them.

"Ms., you have to step back and let us search," a police officer said.

"Murder," another officer said, showing her the warrant to search for the murder weapon.

They ransacked the apartment, looking for the gun. They came out with my .357 and a key of heroin and $250,000 in cash.

"Bingo," they said.

"Take his ass to jail!"

"Baby, call the lawyer."

"I'm on it."

***

Slim

The police brought me to Central lock up. A black chubby chick processed me and gave me a red band. They drove me to the Old Parish prison. The police walked me through the double glass doors.

"What he on?" the C.O. asked.

"Murder!" the police said.

"Name?" the female C.O. asked.

"Soulja Slim." The slim brown-skinned chick with long blonde weave looked up at me and smiled.

"I already know his name."

"Where you want him?" the police asked.

"In the first holding tank.

She came around and locked the door. Joy was her name; she was out the Calliope. I was fucking her friend Pam back in the day. Besides, I been running through the Old Parish, so they know me by name in this motherfucker.

A tall brown-skinned nigga with a bald head came opening the door.

"Nigga, you back again," Sgt. Dark said.

"Yea, you know how them New Orleans folks is."

"What you on?"

"Murder." He shook his head. "Okay, get the bed roll and follow me."

"Where y'all putting me?"

"B1."

"Okay. That's where y'all always putting me."

"Yea, there's a lot of your uptown people in there." I had known Dark ever since I been coming back here when he was a C.O. and now he was a sergeant.

It was dark when I walked on the tier. The tier rep came out. A red bald nigga with tattoos all over him.

"What's up, Slim?"

"Nothing, coolin."

"Your cell right chere. I'll holla at you in the morning." They popped my cell. I put my stuff on the middle bunk, climbed in it and fell asleep.

I got up the next morning, seeing everybody in line for chow.

I didn't feel like eating. I walked over to the phone, calling my girl to see what's good.

You have a collect call from Slim.

"Hey, babe."

"What they talking about?"

"You got a probation hold. The lawyer coming to see you today. I put two hundred on your books."

"Okay."

"Put me on the visitation list."

"I got you." I hung up with her and called Tre.

"Woo. Nigga, what's up?"

"Them bitches kicked in my door last night."

"What! What they got you on?"

"Murder."

"Damn! Okay, I'll hold it down out here. Anything you need, just say the word."

"Good looking."

"I'ma tell Len."

"Do that."

"Later."

Thirty minutes later, the C.O was calling my name over the speaker.

"Morris Brown. Court."

I got dressed, walked to the door. A light-skinned chubby lady patted me down and put handcuffs and shackles on me. Her and a male C.O. walked me to the docks. They took the handcuffs and shackles off me and put me in the holding cell. I walked in and sat on the bench. Not even ten minutes passed before the lawyer came calling my name.

"Morris Brown."

"Right chere." The C.O. walked me to the visitation room. The lawyer came through on the other side. We was going through my paperwork.

"What's the deal?" I asked. Franks Shoes was one of the best murder lawyers in the city. I had paid him thirty grand to just be on standby. I knew down the line I was going to need him.

"Well, Mr. Brown, you on murder charge."

"For who?"

"They said you killed somebody in broad daylight."

"I don't do shit."

"Okay. You got a probation hold, so they going to deny your bond but we can shoot for it anyway."

"What about my money they took?"

"Well, we can fight for it. Because they had a warrant for the murder weapon, not the drugs and money."

"Okay. I need you to work on that."

"I'm on it. But today we going in here to plead not guilty."

"A'ight. I know how it goes."

The C.O. walked me in the courtroom section C. I sat down next to my lawyer looking over a slim white guy with cheap blue slack, white button-down shirt, black penny loafer. He had white blond hair and wore glasses. He was the one prosecuting the case.

"All rise. Judge Dawn presiding." An older slim black lady came out with gray hair and black robe on.

"Have a seat. Start with you, prosecutor."

"H. James back on the behalf of the prosecutor's office."

"Okay. Begin."

"Mr. Morris is booked on a capital murder and we feel bond should be denied."

"Mr. Shoes."

"My client is not a flight risk."

"Well, he got a probation hold. Yea, an outstanding warrant for violating his parole."

"Well, Your Honor, my client was in the hospital and in a coma for months because he got shot several times."

"Okay, look, the bond is set at a million dollars. Court adjourned."

"Well, you got your bond. You need to get the P.O. to lift the hold."

"Just work on the money for me."

"I got you."

"And holla at the P.O."

"I'm on it." They walked me back to the Old Parish.

I got on the phone calling my girl.

"What happened, babe?"

"Bond set a million. But I got this bitch ass parole hold and I know his bitch ass ain't going to lift it."

Well, I'm here, put me on the list."

"I got you."

"Love you."

"And the lawyer going to see if he can get my money back."

"Yea, 'cause we need that."

"You need some money."

"Yea, I need to fix the hole in the door and I want to move."

"Okay. I'm going to tell Tre to shoot you some."

"Okay. Love you."

"Love you back." I dialed Tre's number.

"Woo, what's up?"

"Got a bond but can't go nowhere. The P.O. got a hold on a nigga. But look, I need you to shoot my girl some money when I get off the phone with you."

"I'm on it. I'm going to shoot you a stack on your book."

"Okay. Hold that shit down with my cousin."

"On top of it. You going to be straight when you get out. Tell me what's good. You know what I'm talking about."

"I got you later." I dialed Len's number.

"When you getting out?"

"Got a P.O., might got to do a year."

"Okay."

"I got you put on the visitation."

"Got you."

"Love you."

"Love you, too."

Robert Baptiste

Chapter Eighteen

Tre

Len and I sat in her apartment in the project counting the money and bagging dope up.

I was still fucked up, because they had him back town fighting a fucking murder charge. I was making sure no witness came to court.

"Pass me the blunt," I said.

"What's up with Slim? I thought he was supposed to be getting out?"

"Shit me," I said, hitting the blunt.

"I thought it was sixty days no witness or gun—he would be getting out."

"It suppose' to be."

"I got rid of the gun ."

"He still got a probation hold on him."

"Shit! I forgot about that shit."

"Yea, Kim told me the fucking P.O. not lifting the fucking hold."

"Damn! That's fucked up!" Len said, wrapping the money up.

"How much is that?"

"Ten stacks."

"Okay. That good. We about to score again. What we got left?"

"One key." As I was about to get up to go take a piss, the front door came flying open.

And the fucking N.O.P.D rushed in the apartment, pointing their guns and showing their fucking badges in our faces.

"Get the fuck on the ground."

"I need to see your search warrant," Len said.

"You shut the fuck up and get on the ground," the police said.

"You shut the fuck up. I'm getting on the ground."

The lady police walked in with the warrant showing it to Len. They handcuffed us and sat us on the sofa as they searched the house.

They came from the back with all the money, the two keys and three guns.

"Fuck! When it rains it pours," I said.

"Take their ass to jail," the sergeant said.

"Got you."

They took us to jail, booked us on possession of drugs, money and guns.

I wasn't worried about the state. I just was hoping the feds was not going to come and pick the charges up. They was doing that shit lately in the city.

I called my girl.

"Hello," she said.

You got a collect call from Tre.

"Damn! Nigga, I just told you this shit was going to happen."

"'Man, not now with the preaching shit. I need you to come bond me and Len out. Call the bond man, see how much our bond is."

"Okay."

Three hours later, Len and I walked out the jail. Our bond was $150,000 apiece.

Now my fucking money is fuck up. Lost about $100,000 grand in the house. I paid $300,000 for me and Len to get out.

As I stepped out the shower, I walked in the room and was drying off. Sharon was sitting on the bed.

"Tre, we need to talk."

"Not right now."

"I'm pregnant."

"What!"

"Yes." I walked over to her, sitting on the bed next to her.

"That's good, bae."

"But I'm thinking about having abortion."

"Man, you tripping now."

"No, I'm not."

"Why you want to do that?"

"Man, all this beef shit you into. You not even going to be around when the baby's born."

"Yes, I promise you I will."

"Don't make promises you can't keep."

"So what you want me to do?"

"Get out the street life."

"Okay, look, I just lost four hundred and fifty thousand dollars. I'm broke. When I make it back, I'm out."

"You promise?"

"Yes. I love you."

"Love you," she said, tongue-kissing me.

I took off her clothes, slid my dick into her wet pussy and made love to her all night.

***

Slim

I had been in jail for sixty days. I haven't been to court. They kept setting the court day back. No witnesses have been coming and they haven't found the gun. In New Orleans we have a no ratting rule. You come to court and a nigga going to kill your whole family.

"Morris Brown. Visitation."

I sure hope this lawyer tell a nigga about to go home and they dropped the charges.

"The bitch ass P.O. suppose' to come see me today too. Hope his ass releases the parole hold, so I can fight the charges from the outside."

I walked out on the visitation room. Seeing my lawyer sitting there, I sat down picking up the phone.

"What's good?" I asked.

"Well, I got good news and bad news ."

"Okay, what's good?"

"They dropped the charges."

"And the bad?"

"The P.O. is downstairs."

"Shit! What about the money?"

"I got the check."

"Okay, give it to my girl."

"Okay. Got you." Just then the P.O. walked up to the visitation booth. My lawyer got up and moved over.

"Mr. Brown. How are you?"

"I'm in jail."

"I see. On murder charges."

"They dropped them," my lawyer said.

"Okay, they don't mean you didn't do it. But that's not why we are here. I been had a warrant out for you nine months ago."

"Man, I was in a coma in the hospital."

"You could have got somebody to call. But anyway I'm violating you and giving you a year."

"Damn! Man, you ain't shit. Fuck! Let me talk to my lawyer." *Bitch ass nigga.* He got up and walked off.

"Man, make sure you give that to my girl."

"I got you."

"Later." I walked on the tier, calling my girl.

"Hello," she said.

"His bitch ass gave me a year. But they dropped the charge, and the lawyer coming to see you. He got the money."

"Okay. Love you."

"Love you too." I hung up the phone, dialing Tre's number.

"Woo, nigga. I been waiting for you to call."

"What's up?"

"Man, the police ran in Len house."

"What?" '

"Yea, got me for everything."

"Fuck!"

"Well, that's the attitude that got you in there in the first place."

"Yea, shit fuck up out chere. Fuck! This bitch ass nigga give me a year."

"You think your cousin going to fuck with me?"

"Probably not. Not without me."

"Fuck! I got to make a couple moves."

"Okay, look, give that bitch Pretty some money so that hoe can bring me a cell phone and drugs."

"I got you."

"Later." I walked to the cell with my head fucked up.

Robert Baptiste

Chapter Nineteen

Tre

I stepped out the car in the projects with a couple ounces of dope to make me some money.

I walked down the courtway. I saw Pretty walking toward me.

Pretty was a thick redbone, with tattoos all over her. She had hazel eyes, long black hair, and big red big lips.

She was a slut in the projects. She fuck any niggas with money and killing. Slim and I been fucking her. She about her money. Once you giving her money or weed, you could have your way with her.

She worked back town at the jail. She'd been helping niggas in the project for years to bring shit in the jail.

"What's up?" I said, walking up to her. "I need you to bring Slim something back town for me."

"I'm going to charge you five hundred dollars."

"Cool." I handed her the package and five hundred."

"Now I need you to blow something with me."

"I'm with you?"

I didn't find it weird that she wanted to mix business with pleasure. We went in her house, sat on the couch, popped a few pills, and smoked. The next thing I know she had her head down sucking my dick.

"Yea, suck this dick," I said, laying back, smoking on a blunt, letting her do her thing.

She raised up, taking off her clothes. She climbed on top me, riding my dick in a reverse cowgirl.

"Yea, ride that dick," I said, gripping her titties.

"Fuck! I'm coming," she said, shaking.

I bent over on the couch, fucking the shit out of her with my finger all in her asshole as she came back to back.

I gripped her waist, thrusting in and out of her as I shook. "Fuck! I'm coming." I shot all my hot nut inside her wet pussy. We fell on the couch, catching our breath.

***

Slim

The next night Pretty came to work at the Old Parish prison. She called me off the tier.

"What's up, Pretty?"

"Here, your stuff."

"Good looking out. Tre pop you off?"

"Yea. You need to let me know when you come home. When you get out?"

"I got you in twelve months."

"You going to stay down here or go upstate?"

"I don't know. They don't tell me."

"Okay, I'll find out for you."

"A'ight."

"What you on?"

"Probation hold."

"I'll check into it for you."

"Later." I walked in my cell, opened the box and got on the phone calling my cousin's number.

"What's good?" he asked.

"Man, I'm jail. Got a year to do."

"Damn! Cousin, I'll shoot you something."

"Man, I need you to look out for my man."

"Na, I'm not fucking with that until you get out."

"Damn! Cous."

"Yea, that's how I roll. So holla at me when you get out."

"Okay. Later."

"Later."

I dialed Bond's number, trying to see what the album was doing.

"What's up, Slim?"

"Man, what's good? How the numbers doing?"

"The album sales are doing alright. It sold a hundred thousand dollars in the first month."

"Cool."

"Well, the label not happy with you."

"I know."

"Slim, that's what I been trying to tell you. You got to chill."

"Bond man. This is my life. This is what inspires my lyrics."

"I hear you."

"Later. "

I hit Tre up.

"What's good?" Tre said.

"Cous said no."

"It's cool. I'm just going to have to hit a few licks."

"Okay, nigga, keep your head up."

"Later."

Chapter Twenty

Slim

Here I'm two weeks later riding the white bus heading to Hunt's Correctional. I didn't even get a chance to tell my girl either. They just came and told me to pack up about three in the morning. Me and a couple more niggas.

We pulled up to Hunt's less than an hour. It wasn't nothing but forty minutes from the city. Hunt's was the second largest prison in Louisiana; Angola was first. Hunt's is where you go to get processed in or you can do your time there or be moved to another prison.

As we stepped off the bus, Hunt's correctional officers were standing there in black and red uniform engraved with *Hunt's Correctional* in red writing.

The C.O. took all of us to the barber shop where they cut all our hair and facial hair off. Then took us to the showers that were cold, gave us the bed rolls and brought us to our dorm.

When I walked in the dorm a nigga named Rell came up to me.

"What' up, Slim?" he said, dapping me off.

"What's up, Wootay?"

"Nothing, coolin." Rell was of medium build, short, brown-skinned with a mouth full of golds, and he used to run around the project robbing niggas getting load. They was going to kill him; that's why he stopped hanging in the project.

"What you on?"

"Violation. And you?"

"Nigga got bust with a half of coke and gun. I got five years."

"You doing it here?"

"Na, going to Allen."

"My paperwork said the same here."

Two weeks later, we was pulling upstate to Allen Correctional Prison. Allen was up north around Monroe. This is where a lot of these country niggas at that don't like niggas from the city.

After I got processed in, the C.O. brought me to the dorm. When I walked in, some dark-skinned nigga with gold in his mouth walked up to me. He was wearing blue jeans, blue shirt with white writing on his shirt that read *Allen* on it.

"Where you from, Slim?" he asked.

"Nigga, where the fuck you from?" I said. I know the nigga wasn't from the city, the way he talk. I don't fuck with them Baton Rouge or country ass nigga.

"It not like that."

"Then what it is like?" Some black ass nigga walked up to me. Then I saw who it was: Pee Wee out my project. He stay on the other side of the project on Magnolia.

"What's up, Wootay?" he said.

"Nigga. Pee Wee, what you doing in this bitch?"

"Manslaughter. I took a plea for ten."

"Oh, who that nigga?"

"A country boy from Shreveport."

"Oh."

"Fuck that boy." I followed him to the cut where all the niggas from the city were hanging out. They were chilling in the cut smoking weed, talking on a cell phone or watching TV.

He introduced me to all the niggas. They were from all different parts of the city. Nigga gave me a package and a knife.

"This your bunk," Pee Wee said.

"Okay."

"You know how this shit goes. It's all about the city."

"Yea, I been in Angola."

"Okay."

"Nigga, give me the cell phone and a pack humps."

Before long, I called my girl.

"Hey. They sent me upstate to Allen."

"Okay. I'll send you some money."

"Okay, love. I love you."

"I love you too."

Chapter Twenty-One

Tre

As I sat on the porch in the Iberville Projects around one in the morning smoking a cigarette, I was thinking about how I could get the money to pay the connect. I know Slim said he was cool until he come home, but I don't like owing a motherfucka shit; it don't set right with me.

Who knows, this nigga might wig out and put some change on my head.

I was down to my last couple ounces, and niggas in the city got some fuck up dope. That shit been stepped on a couple times. And they want $80,000 for that bullshit. I wasn't about to pay for that shit. I was thinking about going a jack move and jack one of these bitch ass niggas in the city. I been pushing dope back here even though I moved my girl from here. I helped her get a condo in Slidell. I know a lot of niggas in the 4th ward by doing time with them. As I was about to go inside, I spotted this nigga Joe creeping by this bitch Ashley house. I don't know that nigga was home. I don't forget the nigga shot at me. I'm going to get his ass.

I waited for him about an hour. I spotted him coming out of her house about two in the morning. I grabbed my .357 off my lap and watched him heading to his car. I ran through the cut before he could make it to his car. I came out the dark cut, busting him up. I shot him in the head. As his body fell to the ground, I stood over him shooting him a couple more times in the body. I ran through the cut going to the apartment, going inside.

***

"Bitch ass nigga thought he was going to get away with that? Fuck him." Ten minutes later, I looked out the window; they had police with yellow tape around his body with a lot of people outside looking at them.

The police was going to different people's houses trying to find a witness. But nobody was talking.

***

Slim

I was sitting on the yard smoking a camel hump cigarette. I call them penitentiary cigarette. I was writing this rap. I was rapping it to myself. I was loving the hook:

"My jacket consists of battery, armed robbery, and murders / I'm the realist nigga you hear of since Pac, got it on lock from the streets to the cell block / You bitch, you, Soulja Slim and his committed come to get you / My Mac Fifty will split you in half.

"What's up, Slim?" Pee Wee said, walking up.

"Nothing, writing this rap. Tell me what you think about this hook: *My jacket consists of battery, armed robbery and murders / I'm the realist nigga you hear of since Pac, got it on lock from the streets to the cell block.*"

"I like that." Just then Rell came on the yard, walking up to us. "Man, y'all know that boy got smoked last night in Iberville?."

"Yea," Pee Wee said.

I know already when they said he got smoked; I know who did it.

"Yea, his ass shouldn't have got caught slipping. Fuck him!"

"You know how it goes in the city. Nigga catch you slipping, your ass is dead."

"Morris Brown—visitation," the C.O. said on the speaker.

"I'm going to fuck with y'all later."

I ran in the dorm, jumped in the shower. When I got out, I put on my black Girbaud jeans, white wife beater, and black Reeboks. In here you can dress like you in the free world. All you got to do is get your people to send you a package.

Kim, Len, Mother and Tre send me one every week.

I told Tre to bring my girl and my mother up here to see me.

I walked in the visitation room showing them my ID. I saw Kim looking good as a motherfucker with some tight blue jeans, red button-down shirt, and some red stilettoes with her hair hanging down to her back. Her lipstick was red and looking good on her big lips. I walked up to her, kissing her. She was smelling good. Like Chanel perfume.

"Hey, baby, I miss you," she said.

"I miss you too," I said, kissing and hugging her.

I hugged my mother and my nigga Tre.

"Hey, son. You looking like you gaining weight."

"A little bit."

"What up, boy? How they treat you in here?"

"Been holding it down like a big dog suppose'." We went and sat at the table, eating chicken and pizza.

"Man, you know Pee Wee and Rell in here too."

"Yea, them niggas got a lot of time?"

"No."

"Baby, you got that money?"

"Yea."

"Mom, you good?"

"You know me, I'm making it. Always worrying about you and your brother. Speaking of your brother, he asked about you. He told me to tell you to chill the fuck out."

"Tell him I said what up!"

"Baby, let's go take some pictures."

"A'ight." She leaned her ass on me, causing my dick to get hard.

"Damn! I miss the feeling there," she said, sliding her hand back, feeling my dick.

I took some pictures with my mother and my partner.

"Visitation over with," the C.O. hollered.

I dapped Tre off, hugged my mother, then hugged and kissed my girl.

"Hold it down, my nigga. I'll be waiting for you to get out."

"Same here, stay down. I'll let them niggas know I still got you out there."

"You know I got this."

"Son, be good in here," said Mama.

"I got this, mom."

"Baby, I love you," Kim said, kissing me and hugging me. "I 'll be waiting for you to come home."

"I love you." I watched as they walked out the visitation room.

They made us get naked and bent over, spreading our ass cheeks and lifting our feet, and opening our mouths. This was to make sure a nigga ain't brought shit back.

Chapter Twenty-Two

Slim

Summer 2000

I was working in the field in the hot sun. The state of Louisiana was talking about letting people go home, because the prison was too overcrowded.

They were talking about letting first-time offenders go on probation and parole people out. Shit! I'm ready to get the fuck out.

Tre and everybody was talking about how Cash Money had the city on fire. How Cash Money had the Magnolia and uptown on fire. Tre was telling me how Vamp, Stone, Charley Brown, and a bunch more niggas had the project popping.

He told me Juvenile really had the city on fire and holding it down.

I know I might get on with him and make him do a feature with me.

As I was coming out the field, Pee Wee came up to me.

"Nigga, they got your name on the roll out paper."

"What! Nigga, stop playing," I said, walking up to the board, looking at it.

I saw my name. I was happy as fuck.

The C.O. went to calling people's names, telling them to package their shit.

I jumped in the shower. I stepped out, putting on state blue jeans, blue shirt, and black boots.

I don't want my people to know. I want to surprise them.

My mother moved out of the projects and rented a house in Bunker Hill.

But she still kept the project for me.

The C.O. rolled us to the Greyhound Bus Station.

I waited outside, smoking on a hump and thinking about my plan I was going to execute when I hit the city.

***

Slim

Back in the city, I stepped off the bus, smelling the city's fresh air. It's nothing like New Orleans. I don't care where you go; if you from here, you going to always want to come back here. It's just something about this raggy motherfucker people love.

I thought about calling somebody. But fuck it. I walked to the project. It wasn't nothing but twelve blocks. I need to get my mind right. I thought the whole way there about getting my own label. I was tired of splitting money and getting dropped from labels.

I just need to come up with the money, and it costs millions to run a label.

I walked past the Melpomene projects hoping a nigga ain't spot me and lit my ass up. Then I walked down Simon Bolivar, crossed Jackson passing the Rochambeau Hotel where niggas take them hoes after the club. I walked to Shakespeare Park across the Washington and walked into the Magnolia. I walked in my mother's old apartment. It was hot as hell in there, so I cut the A/C on.

I walked to my bedroom searching for my gun.

I pulled a black .357 out the clothes. I walked in my mother's old room where I put up a 4 half of dope for a rainy day. I need Len to help me break it down and bag it up so I could put some money in my pocket. I was on my ass.

I knocked on her door.

"Who is it?"

"Me, Slim." She opened the door with .380 in hand.

"Damn! Bae, you got out early, huh?"

"Yea."

"When you got out?"

"A couple hours ago."

"Well, I'm glad to see you." We walked to the back bedroom. I fucked the shit out of her.

124

I left her apartment about 3:00 the next morning. I jumped in the shower. I got out, dressed and snorted a line of dope. I left the dope over at Len house so she could mix up for me.

I walked outside, saw Craig in the courtway and asked him to give me a ride to my girl's house.

"Nigga, I know you happy to be free."

"Nigga, you already know."

"So what you going to do now?"

"Shit, try to hit me a lick and get money."

"What about the rap shit?"

"I got to let it go until a nigga can get money."

"I feel you."

"Tell that nigga Tre I'm home and he should get at me."

"A'ight."

***

I walked into my girl's apartment; she wasn't there. She must be working overtime at the hospital. I went in the kitchen hungry as shit. I grabbed some leftover red beans and rice with some fried chicken, warming it up in the microwave. I sat at the table eating it, thinking about how I had to go see my P.O. in 72 hours.

After I finished eating, I walked to the bedroom grabbing me some fresh dark blue Girbauds that still had the tag on them. I added a long white Polo shirt, a black wife beater and some Polo boots.

I walked to the bathroom, took off my clothes, and got in the shower.

It felt so good. A couple minutes later the shower curtain came back. It was Kim standing there.

"Boy, when you came home?" she asked, smiling.

"A couple hours ago."

"Why you didn't call me?"

"I want to surprise you."

"Now what if I had a man over here ."

"Well, I would have fuck both y'all up."

"I'm just playing."

She took off her clothes, getting in with me. She started kissing me. I went down on her in the shower, eating her out. I turned her around, eating her asshole and pussy out from the back as she moaned coming all in my mouth.

I slid my rock-hard dick into her from the back as I slammed her on the ass, pulling her ponytail.

"Fuck! I miss this dick. I'm coming!" she said, with her whole body shaking. "I love you."

As she backed her ass up on me, I couldn't hold back. I shot my hot nut all in her pussy."

"Fuck! I love you, Kim."

Chapter Twenty-Three

Slim

The next day Kim took me to the dealership where I cop a black on black Tahoe. I wanted something new. The summer was about to come. I need something to floss on these niggas. To let them know the big dog was home.

I have the $100,000 advance money left.

Plus I know I make a few dollars off the album. I needed to see about that money.

I left the dealership. Went straight to see the P.O. I walked in to sign the paper.

"What's your name?" the secretary asked.

"Morris Brown."

"Okay, have a seat. He'll be out shortly to see you." Ten minutes later a tall black bald guy came out dressed in a white shirt, black jeans and brown shoes.

"Morris Brown."

"Right chere."

"Follow me to the back." I followed him to his office where I sat across from him.

"I see you been back and forth to prison. I need for you to get a job."

"I got a job."

"What you do?"

"I'm a rapper. My name is Soulja Slim."

"Okay, then. I need for you to pay forty-five dollars a month and take drug testing every month. You fail to report or fail a drug test, you going back to prison. You got three more years on probation. Can you piss?"

"Yea." I stood up in the bathroom as he watched me piss. I handed him the cup; he looked at it on the test side.

"It's good. Next month I'll see you." I walked outside, jumped in my truck, grabbed the blunt out the ashtray, lighting it up as I pulled off.

As I rode back to the projects, I called Bond's number.

I want to check on this record deal and my money. Because the only money I had was the check the police gave me and this record money.

I just blew 60K on this truck. So a nigga need to come up with a plan fast.

"Hello," he said.

"Whoo. What's good on the money from the label?"

"They got your money."

"Okay, I'm going to hit them up."

"Yea, man, when you going to get it together?"

"Man, look, I think we going to need to separate for now because we not working out. You keep preaching to me."

"Because a nigga want to see you win."

"My nigga, I'm not going to change this me. A hustler. Soulja."

"Okay, look, I'm not going to give up on you. But I'm going to let you do *you*. But remember them streets never let go. You going to always be in and out prison until you get yourself together. And you going to miss out on a great thing fucking with them streets. You might need to start your own shit."

"Yea, I been thinking about that. I might just do that."

"Okay, holla at me."

"Later." I stopped in the project first before I headed to Baton Rouge. Tre was in the circle hustling. I walked up to him, dapping him off.

"Glad you home, my nigga."

"Yea, me too."

"Shit, what you got going on?"

"Shit, trying to put something together."

"You need holla at cous."

"Yea, I will. Just let me get some money together."

"For sure."

"Look, I got to push. I'm going to get up later."

"Later."

I walked in the office at *No Limit*. Rob was sitting in there.

"What's good, Slim?"

"Here about my check."

"Yea, I got it right here."

"I heard y'all talking about dropping me, huh?"

"Well, we can't right now. You owe us another album." He slid me a check for $300,000.

"Your album almost went gold. It sold four hundred thousand. We took out everything from advance money and promotion."

"Okay."

"Man, Slim, you got talent. You just got to let that street shit go. You one of the biggest stars in New Orleans."

"Look, the streets made me. This who I am. Take it or leave it."

"Hear you."

"Later."

***

Slim

I sat on the sofa at Kim's apartment, smoking, thinking about what I should do with the money. I was at a crossroads, thinking if I should score some dope from my cousin or should I save and put it into the album because I owe the label another one. And it was on me to come up with the money.

Just then Kim walked into the apartment with groceries in her hand.

"What's wrong with you?"

"Nothing, just thinking."

"About what?"

"Shit. I just got a check from the album."

"Okay."

"I was thinking about buying some heroin because this all I got left."

"Or what else?"

"I owe them another album."

"How much is the check?"

"Three hundred thousand dollars."

"Okay, what you should do is pay for your album and studio time and double your money. Fuck the dope. I believe in you."

"You right, bae. I'm going to give you a hundred and fifty thousand dollars for a rainy day and invest the rest in myself.

"I love you," she said, kissing me.

"I love you too."

We went to the bedroom. We took off our clothes. I proceeded to make love to her.

I sucked on her rock-hard nipples, then I kissed and sucked on her stomach. I spread her legs, sucking and licking her hard pearl tongue as she moaned holding my head down.

"Yes, baby, don't stop. I'm coming." She came back to back in my face.

I raised up, slid my dick in her wet pussy and stroked her softly.

"I love you, Slim."

"I love you back," I said, tongue-kissing her.

She climbed on top, riding my dick, and biting on her bottom lip as I caressed her titties.

I grabbed her ass, bouncing her up and down on me.

"I'm about to nut."

"Me too." She started riding my dick real fast, as I gripped her ass coming inside of her as she came all over my dick and stomach.

***

Slim

After I made love to Kim, I got up, took a shower, got dressed and left her asleep.

I thought about what Kim said.

I need to start investing in my own music after this album. I'm not signing to nobody else. I'ma do my own fucking thing.

I pulled up to Mike's house.

I hit him up letting him know I needed beats. I had the $100,000 advance money, plus $300,000 I got from the album.

But don't get this shit twisted. If I can hit me a nice lick for some bricks and like a half million ticket, a nigga ass is got.

I walked in the house. Mike was putting the beats together.

"What's up, nigga? Glad to see you home," he said, dapping me.

"I'm glad to see you too."

"I heard they don't drop you."

"Yea, I still owe them another album."

"Well, let's get to work. Everything on me."

"What!"

"Don't pay for shit."

" No, here's five thousand dollars. Just come up with some beats for me."

"You know I got you."

"A'ight, nigga. I'm out."

"Later."

Robert Baptiste

Chapter Twenty-Four

Slim

I was sitting at the bar in the House of Blues. I just finished ripping the stage up. It was a concert filled with a lot of local rappers. They had a couple major labels looking to sign people. It was cool for them to do this and give niggas and hoes chance to go nationwide like my little Home Girl Magnolia Shorty. A cool little chick out my project.

As I was sitting drinking a Heineken at the bar checking out the fine bitches in the club, somebody tapped me on my shoulder. I looked around, and it was Tracy big fine ass. I had forgot all about her. I hadn't talked to her in years ever since I went to Angola. I had lost touch with her.

She had on some black leggings that showed off her every curve, along with her camel toe. Her matching halter top held in her big titties that showed off her hard nipples. She had a diamond ring in her navel with her hair hanging in deep waves looking good. She had a red LV bag on her shoulder and some red bottom heels on.

"What's good, Slim?" She smiled.

"What's good with you?"

"Nothing. Where you been? Why you ain't called a bitch? You don't fuck with me no more."

"Na, it's not like that. I lost your number and I been in and out of prison. You know how my life is. I just got out."

"Yea, I know. I like how you rip that stage."

"You like that there, huh?"

"Yea. So what you been up to?"

"You know me getting money."

"So you really just got out, huh?"

"Yup."

"So I'm trying to see what that dick hitting for." She smiled.

"Shit, we can do that. Let's go."

I laid back in the hotel bed, watching as this bitch deep- throated my dick like a porn star.

"Fuck! Suck this bitch," I said, as she sucked the tip of my dick head and sucked on my balls.

This hoe was a beast, sucking a nigga dick and sending my eyes rolling in the back of my head and my ass cheeks tight . Then she climbed on top of me and rode my dick in a reverse cowgirl position, as I grabbed her ass bouncing her hard up and down on my dick, as I stuck my finger in her asshole.

"Fuck! Yea. Ooo—Ooo! Shit, dick—dick is so fuckin' good. I'm coming all over this big motherfucker."

I flipped her over, putting her legs on my shoulders and went fucking the shit out of her as she dig her nails into my back. I 'm not going to lie, this bitch got some fire pussy.

"Fuck, Slim, you in my stomach."

"Bitch, this what you want, right?"

"I'm coming again," she said, with her body shaking.

I flipped her over in a doggy style position. I grabbed her ass cheeks and pulled her hair as I thrusted in and out of her as she grabbed the bed sheet, putting her face in the pillow and screaming out my name. That fire bag of dope had me hard as a motherfucker and got me banging this bitch.

I pulled my dick out this bitch wet pussy and slid into her wet asshole. I slowly stroked her asshole as she slid back on my dick. Then I went to fucking her asshole out.

I went to shaking as she rocked back on me, playing with her wet pussy.

"Shit! I'm about to nut," I said.

She pulled my dick out her ass and turned around, sucking it until I shot hot nut all over her face. I see why she went crazy in the club on me. This bitch is a beast.

My cell phone rang, waking me up. I looked over at Tracy's big butt ass.

"Damn! This bitch a motherfucker." I looked at my phone; it was Kim. I didn't even bother to hit her back. I got up, put on my clothes, went to the bathroom and took a piss.

I walked out slapping Tracy on the ass.

"Huh?"

"Come, let's go." She got up, put her clothes on, went to the bathroom and cleaned up.

As we rode to her house in Kenner, I hit the blunt, passing it to her.

"You still fucking with this nigga—Joe?"

"Yea. Why? What's up?"

"I need a lick."

"Nigga, you trying to get me killed fucking with this Jamaican."

"I'm going to get rid of his ass. You ain't got that to worry about anything."

"Okay, let me think about it."

"A'ight, hit your nigga up. I'm going to pop you off." "Okay, Daddy!" she said, kissing me.

I watched as she got out of my truck, going inside with no draws on, her ass bouncing everywhere.

"Damn! That bitch is fine."

***

Slim

I made it to Kim's apartment. She was already gone to work. I got in the shower and changed clothes. I grabbed my gun and headed to the projects.

As I was hitting the 1-10 interstate, my phone rang.

"What's up, love?" I said.

"I was calling because you don't come to my house last night," Kim said.

"Yea, I know. After I left the House of Blues, I went to the studio to work on the album."

"Oh. I was just checking on you."

"Yea. I just left your house taking a shower."

"Oh, where you at now?"

"Going to the projects."

"You be safe."

"Love you."

"Love you back.

Kim ass lucky I'm in love with her. Otherwise, I would have dumped her, especially as she been sweating a nigga and shit. But I love her, so I put up with it.

My phone rang again; it was Mike.

"What's good, nigga?" I asked.

"Shit, I got a couple beats I want you to listen to. Stop through when you get a chance."

"I'm going to hit the project and I'm going to be on my way in a little bit."

"For sure."

"Later." My mom called.

"You wasn't going to tell me you made it home?"

"Sorry, mom, I'm going to come through there later on."

"Okay, son, I'm about to go."

"Love you." I pulled up in the projects going by Len house; she told me she had a few dollars for me.

I walked into her apartment. She was cooking grits, eggs and sausages. Tre was over there bagging up dope high as a motherfucker.

"You want some?" she asked.

"Hell yea. I'm hungry." I went into the bathroom shooting some dope, killing my morning sickness. I came out seating at the table and fucked the food up.

"Nigga, you came up with a lick for us?"

"Man, remember the bitch Tracy?"

"Yea, big bitch out Kenner."

"Yea. That's her. Well, the bitch be fucking with this Joe. That hoe got Kenner on lock. I holla her. She said she might put us on him."

"Fuck that hoe. Let's get him."

"We can do that too."

"I'm with that."

"Let's see what this bitch talking about and we go from there."

"Okay. Sound like a play."

"What you got for me?"

"Five thousand. I need some money for the lawyer."

136

"How much?"

"Ten thousand."

"What he talking?"

"Probation."

"Mine still talking this feds shit. I just give that nigga ten thousand."

"Damn! Key the five and give to the lawyer. I'll bring you the other five. How much dope you got left?"

"Two ounce."

"Okay, if you ain't made the five thousand, call me and let me know."

"Okay."

"I'm about to dip. I got to go holla at Mike on the beat side. I gotta put out another album."

"At time like this, nigga, you worrying about rap."

"Nigga, stop tripping."

"I hear you."

"You coming through tonight? A bitch horny as shit," said Len.

"Yea, I'm coming through and bust you." I smiled, walking out the door.

I sat at Mike's house with my pad I had in Hunt's listening to some of the beats he had made.

"Like this beat? I got something for it."

"Let me hear it." I walked in the booth putting the head phone on, listening to the beat, then I started rapping.

I walked out after laying it down.

"I love that."

"What other beat you got?" I walked in there and laid three more raps down.

"I love it, my nigga. So they sign you to another deal, huh?"

"Yea, two hundred and fifty thousand dollars advance."

"You got to stay out."

"My nigga, you know me better than anybody."

"I know this your life. You never thought about changing."

"I don't."

"But if you going to blow, you got to give one of them up."
I hit the blunt, blowing the smoke out my nose.
"I feel you."
I looked at my phone; it was Kim. I ain't answer back. I ain't been home in a few days. So I know she was going to be on some trip shit. I had too much shit on my plate to deal with.
"I'm going to hit you when I got a few more beats."
"Later."

Chapter Twenty-Five

Slim

I stuck my in the door. I already know Kim was coming with the bullshit, since I been gone almost a week.

As I walked in the apartment, she jumped up pointing her finger in my face.

"Nigga, is you out your fucking mind? Got me worried about and stressing about you. I don't know if you fucking dead or not."

"Man, look, this is my motherfucker life. I'm a grown ass man! I don't answer to you about a fucking thing."

"You probably was fucking one of them nasty ass project bitches."

"Watch out. I just came to get some of my clothes and take a bath."

"Look, you can get your shit and get the fuck out my house."

"Bitch, you ain't saying nothing but a word. I don't need this bullshit. That's why I hate coming to this motherfucker." I grabbed a bag and stuffed my shit in the bag and walked out that motherfucker.

I jumped on the interstate, heading to the projects. I dropped my shit off and headed to Len house.

I knocked on the door and she answered.

"I need a bag of dope. This dumb bitch got on my nerves."

"Who?"

"Who else?"

"Kim."

"You already know." I snorted two bags of dope. I sat at the table in the kitchen, pulling out baby laxative; this is the best shit to cut up dope. When I was done stirring it up, I made a line and snorted some more dope.

"Fuck! This shit fire."

"You got some more pills?" she asked.

"Yea. I got to go to my apartment." As I was about to get up, gunshots went to ringing out in right of her window. I grabbed her and pulled her to the floor. You never know in the projects, a stray bullet could fly through the window. I been ducking bullets like this in the project my whole life in my mother's apartment. A couple times bullets came flying through my mother's window and hit shit in our apartment. After the shooting stopped, I grabbed my .45 looking out the door. I saw Tre and Craig coming out the hallway. I walked into the courtway, meeting up with them.

"Nigga, who that y'all was shooting at?" Tre said.

"Them nigga out the 17th. Fav and them," Craig said.

"Look, I'm about to bounce and go back to Len house. You know the police about to come back chere and make it hot."

I went to my apartment, grabbed the pills. I walked in Len house; she was bagging up the dope.

"Here the pills." I gave her two blue dolphins.

An hour later I had her in the bed in a missionary position fucking the shit out of her as she held her own legs up.

"Yea, daddy, beat this pussy up. I'm coming. Fuck! I'm coming."

"Damn! This pussy good."

"All for you, daddy. I love you." I flipped her over, fucking her from the back as I gripped her shoulders and bit her on the neck.

"I'm coming again. I swear I'm!" she said with her whole body shaking.

As she backed up on me, I went to shaking .

"I'm about to nut," I said.

"Shoot it all in me, Slim." I shot all my nut in her. I fell on the bed trying to catch my breath.

"Fuck! I need that," she said, putting the cover over her ass.

I put my clothes on, leaving her sleeping in the bed. My head was fucked up; a nigga couldn't sleep right. I walked in the kitchen, grabbed the ounce of the table, going outside.

***

Slim

I walked outside looking out the hallway to make sure the police wasn't posted up no more after the shoot-out.

I sat on the porch smoking on dro, serving dope bags and thinking about a hustle I can hit.

It's been a couple days; this bitch Tracy ain't hit a nigga back yet.

The nigga she scoring from—he got Kenner on lock.

The bitch might feel she don't want to turn on the nigga because he been looking out for her.

But the bitch going to make me grab her and the fucking nigga.

"What's up, Slim? You got something?"

"Yea, what you trying to get?"

"Two bags."

"Here." Another fiend walked up.

"Slim, I need something for eighty."

"I give five for the eighty." Just then Kim called my phone.

"What's up, Kim?"

"You just going to leave like that?"

"Huh? Kim, you put me out."

"Slim, how would you feel if I don't come home for weeks at a time?"

"Kim, you know I'm in the fucking streets trying to get money and paying for studio time, pay bills and other shit."

"All I'm asking for you to do is check in with me. So I know you safe."

"Okay."

"Where you at?"

"In the project."

"Okay, I'm coming over there. Later."

"I'ma hit you up. I gotta go finish this album."

"I'ma tell you—if you don't call me, I'm coming back and going to beat one them hoes up. For playing with me."

I laughed.

"I'm serious."

"I know, that's why I'm laughing."

"Okay, you know I cut up before."

"I got you."

"Love you."

"Love you." I hung up.

Kim ass is crazy as shit. But I got to respect her mind because she always be there for a nigga when I go to jail.

Just then Mike hit me up.

"I got some more beats."

"I'm on my way." I jumped in my truck, heading at the parkway.

I sat in his house listening to the beat, writing a rap to it.

I walked in the booth and laid the rap down.

"I like that," Mike said.

"You know they going to feel a nigga every time I come out."

"What you going to name the album?"

"*Streets Made Me.*"

"I like that."

I stayed in the studio with Mike till about two in the morning.

When I was pulling up in the project, Kim's car was parked in the driveway. I walked upstairs going into the house. I had forgot she had a key. My mother gave her one. My mother love Kim. Because she said she got a good head on her shoulders and she not like the rest them bitches in the project. She want her to have a grandchild.

I walked in my room and she was knocked out in the bed. I was going to wake her up, but she looked so good sleeping. I climbed in the bed next to her, laying down next to her. I wrapped my arms around her, kissing her.

Chapter Twenty-Six

Slim

I woke up the next morning with my girl lying next to me looking me in my face.

"Hey, baby," she said.

"Hey, love."

"I told you I was coming over here."

"I know you were when you said you was coming."

"This what I been longing for throughout the last couple of weeks—to wake up with you," she said, smiling.

I pulled her close to me, tongue-kissing her. I eased her thong off, slid my dick in her wet pussy and began to make love to her. I slowly stroked her as I sucked on her hard nipples as she moaned in passion.

"I love you, Kim."

"I love you back, Morris." I pulled out of her, going down to her pussy and sucked and licked on her clit until she came hard with her body shaking. I moved down to her toes, sucking on them. Then I flipped her over on her stomach, kissing her back all the way down to her ass cheeks. She spread her legs, letting me slide my dick in her wet pussy as I laid on top of her and locked as I grind my dick inside her pussy.

"I'm about to come again."

"Me too." She tensed up, so did I as we came together.

"Fuck! It feel so good," she said.

"Yea, it do," I said, laying on top of her with my dick still in her pussy.

We laid there for a while with her head on my chest, watching TV.

"I love you, Slim," she said, getting out of bed.

"Where you going?"

"To take a shower."

"I'm coming." We stood in the shower for another hour making love to each other. When we got out, she cooked us breakfast.

"Baby, I got to go to work."

"Okay, you got money?"

"Yea, I'm straight." I walked her to her car.

"Love you," I said, kissing her.

"Love you too. Be safe. Call me, nigga."

"I will."

"How the album coming?"

"It's almost done."

"Okay. Love you." She kissed me

"Love you back.

I watched as she pulled out the projects.

***

Tre

As I was riding around the city thinking of a lick to hit and wondering if this bitch Tracy had hit Slim back, my phone rang. I smiled when I saw who it was. It was my throwback bitch Pinky from out the East. This bitch straight thug. Always claiming that I'm the father of her youngest baby. But the hoe a lie. One thing about the bitch: she keep G and never trip on me about child support or tell Sharon anything. I used to pop the bitch off. But the hoe only call me when she got a nigga she want me to rob. The hoe straight cut-throat for real and fuck over nigga whether you lame or not. If you not popping her off, she going to get you jacked.

"What's up, Pinky?"

"Come holla at me."

"I'm on my way."

"I hear they damn near killed your ass, huh?"

"Girl, you know they can't kill no Soulja."

"I hear that."

"Later."

I pulled up in a hood with some run-down apartment that looked like the projects. Niggas be slinging big dope back here and getting money.

I jumped out the truck with my 9mm in my hand running upstairs, knocking on her door. She answered with a blunt in her mouth, wearing some boy shorts and a pink wife-beater. She had no shoes on, and Polo pink hat on. She's called Pinky because she look like the porn star.

I walked in looking around. She had a pound of weed on a glass table that she was breaking down along with some money. This bitch had me spook to be in her crib because she sells weed out here and the police can kick this bitch in at any time. I got her out of jail twice when they kicked in her door. That why the bitch don't have her kids now. She went and did state time, and the kids were with the state back then. I think the bitch momma got them now. She got five kids. But all from different niggas.

And all them niggas are in jail or dead.

I fucked with the bitch hard, but she just be on bullshit sometime. And every time I'm around the bitch she want to fuck. That hoe do the same shit I do. Coke, dope, pills and weed. I had met the bitch at a concert back in the day. We fucked on the first night and we been fucking around ever since. She put me on a couple licks and I popped her off; that's how we been rolling.

The hoe ain't shit. Shit don't want shit. All the hoe want to do is get fucked in every hole and roll off pills and get high.

"What's up? You want to hit this?" she said, sitting on the couch with her legs open and passing me dro.

I hit it and started choking.

"Damn! This shit good."

"Look, I need you to rob this nigga Kelly."

"A'ight, what the nigga playing with?"

"A couple bricks."

"What the nigga did you?"

"Beat on me."

"Okay. Where the nigga stay."

"I'll show you."

"Bitch, you prolly did something out of pocket for the nigga to beat your ass."

"Fuck that nigga."

"Fuck him. Where he stay?"

"Come on, I'll show you."

"Na, wait until it get dark."

"Okay."

"Look like your ass rolling off the x-pills."

"You know I'm. Come over here and let me suck that dick of you."

I walked over to her, laid back on the couch and let her go to work.

Before you know it, I had her bent over on the couch fucking the shit out of her. I pulled my dick out and shot nut all over her ass.

She went in the bathroom and cleaned up.

Next twenty minutes we were parked in front of the nigga house in Kenner.

"That his car right there."

"He home."

"Yea."

"Go knock at the door." She got out, walked up to the nigga door, knocking on it. I stood on the side of the house waiting for the nigga to come to the door.

As soon as he opened it, I rushed past her, pointing the gun in the nigga face.

"What going on?"

"Bitch, go get the dope."

"Yea, Daddy." She came back with the two keys of coke and money.

"You bitch." I shot the nigga twice in the head.

Moments later, we sat in her living room smoking weed and counting money.

It wasn't nothing for her to see me kill a nigga. I shot many niggas in front of her.

"How much?"

"Twenty-five."

"Okay, take half."

"Look, give me the money and you take the two keys."

"Bet. I need this score."

"Me too. I love you, nigga."

"Love you too, bitch." I grabbed the two keys and bounced.

Slim, Craig, Len and I sat at Len's kitchen table breaking the two keys.

"Nigga, where you get this lick from?" Slim asked, hitting the blunt.

"One of my old bitches came through for me."

"Who that be like that there?"

"Pinky."

"Damn! Way back, huh?"

"You already know. What's up with Tracy ass?" I asked as I was counting the money.

"I don't know. Let me hit her ass up right now because if I dial the bitch's number, she answers on the first ring."

"Hey, bae."

"Bitch, don't *hey bae* me. What's up on the lick?"

"I got you."

"I'ma be at your house tomorrow."

"Okay."

"A'ight, don't be playing that game."

"I got you, Slim."

"Later."

"What the hoe talking about?"

"Tomorrow I go holla at her."

"Hope this bitch ain't faking."

"Me either."

Chapter Twenty-Seven

Slim

The next day I pulled up to Tracy's apartment in Kenner. I got out with a Glock in my waist line. I walked up to her door knocking on it.

She opened it in some tight black leggings with the matching top and some pink LV slippers with her hair in a ponytail, puffing on a blunt.

"Hey, baby," she said, kissing me. Her eyes were bloodshot.

"I'm cool," I said, walking in looking around.

She had some pills with a couple ounces of dro on the table.

I pulled my gun off my waist and put it on the table.

"What's good? Why the fuck you ain't holla at me? What kind of game you playing?"

"I ain't playing no games. I just came back from Houston for him and dropped off ten keys of coke and heroin."

"So what up with this nigga?"

"Here, hit this shit," she said, passing the blunt.

"What's this?"

"Some Purp from Cal." I hit the blunt and went to choking. Then I hit it again.

"Damn! This shit good. Now what up with the nigga?" I said, passing the blunt back to her."

"First, I want a hundred thousand and a bus ticket out of town."

"A'ight, that's my word ."

"I think the feds about to come down. So I 'm tripping to get out but the nigga talking about I can't get out or he going to kill me."

"Don't trip on that. Now tell about the nigga."

"The nigga run shit in Kenner. He stay around Connect Avenue on Joe Yenny across from the race track. In a big white house with cameras on the house. He keep at least two hundred and fifty in the house along with five bricks of coke and dope. And twenty pounds of weed in the garage."

"Okay. When the nigga home?"

"All days."

"So how we going to get him?"

"I'll help you."

"What's a good time?" Just then her phone rang.

"This him."

"I need you to come make a move tonight."

"Okay." She hung up.

"Tonight. If you trying to make a move."

"Yea."

"Okay. I'm going to hit you up when I go there."

"A'ight."

"Now let's go to the back so you can fuck the shit out me in every hole while I'm rolling on these pills." I walked with her to the back room and got in.

***

Tre

I was laying in the bed getting my dick sucked by Michelle.

"Damn! I'm about to nut," I said, shooting all in her mouth.

"That's what I specialize in," she said, getting up to go to the bathroom.

"You a fucking beast," I said, grabbing the blunt out the ashtray.

Just then my phone rang. I looked over; it was my nigga Slim.

I hope this nigga got something for me. I 'm on my ass and my nut swinging in the sand. Sharon tripping on a nigga, talking about a nigga need to help her with the bills. We just got into it; that's why I been over here by my bitch house. Shit get fuck up when a nigga ain't got no money; bitches get to tripping.

"Woo, nigga, what's up?"

"Nigga, it time to make this move."

"Okay. Woo. I'll meet you in the 'jects."

She walked out the bathroom as I was putting on my clothes.

"Nigga, where you going?"

"I got to go handle some business."

"Man, you always got something to do when it come to me."

"Michelle, you know what kind of nigga I'm and you know what you sign up for."

"I know, but damn—"

"Man, stop tripping."

"Man, you say I'm tripping, but when it come to spending time with me, either Slim want you to do something or Sharon does."

"Man, that's not true. So you still tripping on Sharon."

"Whatever."

"Man, you know I wasn't leaving my girl."

"Nigga, between me, coke, dope and streets you already left your girl."

"I hear you."

"You know I'm not tripping on that shit no more. Get your shit and get the fuck out my house."

"Damn! That's how you feeling." I walked up to her try to hug her.

"Boy, watch out."

"You know I love you."

"Whatever! You make me sick."

"I'm out."

"And nigga, you better come your ass back when you finish."

"I got you," I said, kissing her. I grabbed my strap, walking out the house. I jumped in my Lexus truck.

I pulled up in the project. Slim was waiting on me. I jumped in his truck and he pulled off.

"What's the deal?"

"The nigga Joe."

"Okay." I hit Tracy on the phone.

"Hey."

"You ready?"

"Yea, waiting on you."

***

Slim

We parked two cars down from the house. The plan was we were going to let her go knock on the door. When he answered, we was going to rush in on the nigga. We got out the car with her and hid on the side of the house.

We watched as she walked up to the house knocking on the door.

As he opened it, we rushed in the house.

We pointed our guns in the nigga face.

"What's going on?" he said.

"Nigga, where the fucking dope and money?"

"I don't know what you are talking about."

"Tracy, you know where the shit at?" I asked.

"Yes." I pulled the trigger, shooting him in the back of the head. I watched as his body fell to the floor.

"Now where the shit?" I asked. She walked us to the bedroom.

"He keep it in the wall." I walked up to the wall, tapping on it.

"It's hollow. Go get some hammers."

Tre and I went to knocking the wall down. They had a lot of money and drugs.

"Jackpot," I said, pulling the plastic bags of money and dope out.

We started loading the dope and money in bigger plastic bags.

Then we went in the garage and found ten pounds of weed.

They had a pit bull guarding it, so I shot him.

I went back in the house after loading the stuff in the truck and grabbed the tape out of the camera and smashed out.

***

Slim

We sat in her kitchen counting the money. It was a half million. The lick was big.

"Man, this was a nice lick," Tre said.

"Sure was," I said.

"Thanks to me," Tracy said, hitting the weed. The lick was for 10 bricks of heroin and 20 pounds of weed.

"Nigga, I need mine."

I got up, walked to the bathroom and came back out, shooting her in the head.

"What the fuck!"

"Nigga, grab the shit."

"Damn! Nigga, why you smoke the hoe?"

"Nigga, she told me the feds might be on her and them niggas. If the hoe get caught she might tell the feds about the murder we did. No witness. Let's roll." We grabbed everything and jumped in my truck, pulling off.

***

Peter

When I pulled up to my brother's house in Kenner, police were everywhere. They had yellow and red tape around my brother's house .

I stepped out of the car, walking up to the house.

As I was about to ask the police what was going on, the paramedics were bringing a body out the house.

I ran over to them.

"Is that my fucking brother?" I asked.

They stopped the stretcher and pulled back the sheet so I could see.

"What happened?" I asked the police.

"Looks like a home invasion. We found drugs and money in different suitcases in the closet."

Damn! Somebody jack my brother, I thought to myself.

"Did you know he was selling drugs?"

"No. I didn't."

As I peeped in the house, I saw blood everywhere.

The dog was dead on the floor.

I walked to my car, pulling off.

I pulled off thinking about my brother.

We came over here from Jamaica, poor as dirt. He built this drug shit from the grown up. We moved here to New Orleans, because you make a lot of money off the heroin, but at the same time we got family down here.

After the police left, I went back to the house.

I looked around and saw blood everywhere.

I walked in the bedroom looking at the picture of us on the nightstand. Tears started falling from my eyes.

He was my right-hand man.

As I tore the picture out of the frame, putting it in my pocket, I dialed a few Jamaicans I know in the city.

This was my cousin.

"Yea, some niggas killed my baby brother."

"Don't worry, we going to get them."

"Okay." I hung up the phone, walked out the house, jumped in my car, pulling off with tears in my eyes. I was on a mission. I was going to kill these niggas myself.

Chapter Twenty-Eight

Slim

We sat in Len's apartment breaking down and bagging up. I had split everything with Tre down the middle. We going to break a couple these bricks down and hustle and get my cousin his money. I made a couple lines, hitting the dope.

"Fuck! This shit is good," I said, leaning back.

Tre shot in his vein.

"Fuck! This dope is good."

"I see you nigga came back up. Huh?"

"You know I wasn't going to stay down." Tre leaned over on the table.

"Nigga, you good?" I asked. He didn't say shit.

"Tre nigga, you good."

"Fuck! This nigga, don't OD in this fucking house."

Fuck! I was alarmed. My high was blown. "Come help me bring this nigga to the tub."

Len helped me carry this nigga to the bathroom. I turned on the cold water.

"Go get some ice." Len brought me some ice back. I put it under his nuts and arm pit, trying to shock this nigga back.

"Go to the store and get some icy!" I told Len.

***

Len

I ran outside going to get in the car as dope fiend Alice came walking up to me. She always begging me for money.

"Len."

"Not right now."

"I got twenty-five. Where Slim at?"

"Shit! Alice, Tre OD in my house. In fact, come help me get some ice bags."

We came back together. She helped Slim and I put ice all over Tre, trying to bring him back. This shit helped too when Slim ass OD outside. We had to do the same thing for him.

Ten minutes later, Tre shook back.

"What the fuck happen?" he said, with his eyes opening wide.

"Nigga, you went out," Slim said.

"You got some more that shit?" Alice asked.

"Yea, give her two bags for me," Slim said.

We helped the nigga get out the bath.

"Man, this cold!" he said.

"I told you that shit going to take both niggas away from here."

"I got this."

"Yea, that's why your ass was OD in my tub."

"Whatever."

Next thing I know—I had dope fiends knocking at my door, looking for the dope Tre OD on.

***

Slim

I sat on the porch serving motherfuckers. I had a welfare line. All it took was a motherfucker to hear that nigga OD on some dope then it's on and poppen.

I caught the raw selling 20 bags of dope. I made $15,000 in a couple hours from selling bags and grams.

Craig walked up, dapping me off.

"Nigga, I heard we back."

"Yea, it's all love." I finished serving the dope fiends. Then I went inside, giving him a 4 half of dope.

"Bring me twenty thousand back."

I was going to sell the bricks for $120,000. But I thought again. I need all the money.

"Got you." Just then Mike hit me on the phone.

"What up, nigga? How's the album doing?"

"Okay, I need to put some more songs on it."

"Okay, I got some beats."

"I need to turn on the album. Let me call you back."

I hung up and called him back.

"What's good?"

"What you got for me?"

"I'm halfway finished with the beat.

"Okay, shoot it to me when I come."

"A'ight, I got you." Just then My P.O. called.

"Hey, what up?" I asked

"We need to talk. You ain't been here to see me in a minute."

"Yea, I been out of town doing a show."

"Well, you didn't ask me if you could go. We need to talk."

"Okay, I'll be there."

"Don't make me put a warrant out on you, Mr. Morrison."

"I got you. I'll come in tomorrow."

"Bye."

That nigga got me fuck up. I'm not going there even if he lock my ass up. I'm dirty too. I ain't got time to fuck with him; he'll have to come get me out the Nolia. I pulled up to Mike's house. I got out and dapped a few niggas off on the park way.

"What's up, Slim?" Shaw said.

"Cool, about to go and finish this album.

"Okay, that nigga in there."

I sat in the chair, lighting a cigarette up.

"Mike, I need a bounce beat."

"I got you." I rolled a blunt up, listening to the beat. Then I wrote the song on, and I walked in the booth laying it down as I hit the blunt rapping it.

"You like that there?"

"Yea, nigga, it was cool."

"Yea, something to make them hoes shake their ass to."

"I feel you. You need a club banger."

"I need you to mix it down and send it the label asap"

"When you trying to put the album out?"

"Shit around the summer. You know that when shit be jumping."

"Nigga, you going to stay out for this album."

"Man, you know me. I got to stay tooled up, got so much beef in the streets."

"Man, you got to slow down if you want to win with this rap shit."

"Man, this rap shit comes second to the streets. I got make sure a nigga not trying to kill me."

"Feel you."

I stayed there a couple more hours listening to beats and putting raps to them.

Chapter Twenty-Nine

Tre

Michelle and I pulled up to this BMW dealership. I was going to use her name and credit to get the car. She just wanted me to take her shopping.

"Baby, you must have hit a lick."

"Yea, you know how I do."

"I told your ass you need to before."

"I got this."

"You see what happened to Slim."

"Please I get enough preaching at home."

"I'm just saying.

Just then a bald white man came out of the office.

"Can I help you?"

"Yea, I want to get this BMW."

"Okay, it's going to cost you."

"Money no problem."

We stood in the office about an hour.

Then we rode off the lot in the car.

We walked around the mall as she bought LV purse, bags and shoes. Along with *Victoria's Secret* stuff.

"Come on, baby let's go get something to eat." We sat in the food court talking and eating.

"So when are we moving in together?"

"Move in?"

"You said once you got your money right, we were moving in together."

"Man, I'm not leaving my girl."

"What, nigga! You been lying all this time to me."

"You know what you was getting into."

"So what? I'm just your side bitch?"

"Man, stop it."

"Stop what? Nigga, I thought you love me."

"I do. But that don't mean I'm leaving my girl."

"Well, fuck that! Take me home."

"You think I'm about to leave my girl? And she pregnant."

"Take me home."

"Come on."

As I pulled up to her spot, my phone rang. It was Kim.

"So what you going to do?" she asked me.

"I got to take this."

She got out my car, slamming the door.

"What's up, Kim?"

"Your girl is about to have the baby."

"I'm on my way."

***

Tre

I stood in the hospital room watching my girl pushing out the baby boy.

"Push, baby. Push, baby," I said.

"Push. Push, Ms. Wilson," the doctor said.

As she pushed, the baby came out. I saw his head, then his body, then his feet. He was all different colors. They wrapped him in the sheet and the nurse took him to be weighed.

She cleaned him up and brought him back to Sharon.

"Here. He weighs five pounds and two ounces."

Sharon held him on her chest, looking at him smiling.

"Hey, Tray Jackson Jr," she said, kissing him.

I smiled; he was named after me.

"You want to hold your son?"

"Yes."

I held him. He felt like a little loaf of bread in my hands.

"Hey, little man," I said, smiling at him.

Then Slim came into the room.

"There goes your Uncle Slim.

"What up, little man?" Then the rest of Sharon's family came in and it was time for me to go.

"I'm glad to see you still alive to see your son," her mother said.

"Mom, don't start," said Sharon.

"I'm out, Baby. Love you," I said, kissing Sharon on her forehead.

Robert Baptiste

Chapter Thirty

Slim

I was sitting at this whole in the wall club called Xscape's on Claiborne where a lot of niggas get killed. Trina, my little bitch, had hit me up and said she wanted to chill. I wasn't doing shit. My album was about to come out. My singles *Make It Bounce For Me*, and *Shit Real* was doing their thing in the city; people was waiting for the album to drop.

"Baby, what been up with you?" she asked me, sipping on her drank.

"Me coolin' working on my album."

"Well, I moved to Kenner."

"Yea, you changed your number."

"Yea, people went to saying I'm the one got them niggas killed around there. So I moved and changed my number."

As she was talking, I saw a couple niggas with tattoos in their face coming toward me. I put my hands on my Glock. They went to booth me up.

I didn't even know them niggas.

Then they walked out of the club.

"Come let's go?" I said to Trina.

"What's going on?"

"Let's go!"

As we were coming out the club, the niggas opened fire, busting at me. I ducked down. Trina went to running. I ran on the side of the car, hitting back fiercely. I lost no time in jumping inside my truck. I smashed out jumping over curves and everything, trying to get the fuck out there.

Niggas was still heading at my truck.

As I hit the bridge heading to Kim's house, I pulled over checking myself. Good thing I had my vest on.

I stepped out the truck in front of Kim's house, checking myself again and then my truck; everything was cool. I had to calm down.

I don't need my girl acting crazy when I walked inside with all these fucking questions.

When I walked in, Kim was knocked out asleep.

I took my clothes off and got in the bed thinking about who the fuck that was that got at me around Xscape.

***

Ham

Tonie and I ran back to the car, jumping in and smashing out.

"Fuck, we miss that nigga!" I said, mad as hell.

"I know," Tonie said

"Damn! We had that nigga so close."

"That nigga must got nine lives or God with him."

We rode around looking for this nigga uptown.

Just then my phone rang; it was Death.

"What's up, niggas?" I heard y'all was shooting at somebody."

"Yea, that bitch ass nigga Slim."

"Did y'all hit the nigga?"

"Fuck no. That nigga got nine lives."

"Yea, y'all hit a couple innocent people. It on the news."

"Damn!"

"Where you at now?"

"Riding around uptown looking for the bitch ass nigga."

"Fuck! We going to catch him later. Come back to the eighth ward. Later."

"Later, my nigga."

"Who was that?" Tonie said.

"Death."

"What he talking? A couple innocent people got hit?"

"We need to call it a night."

"Cool. We gonna catch the nigga."

"Yea, you right. New Orleans too small."

***

Michelle

"Yes, Tre, give me that dick! Don't stop. I'm coming."

"Damn! This pussy good," he said, shaking, nutting all in my wet pussy.

"Damn! I need that," I said, getting up to go to the bathroom when my phone rang. I looked over it and it was my uncle.

"Hello," I said.

"Somebody killed your uncle Joe."

"What! When?"

"A few days ago."

"What happened?"

"Some niggas ran in his house, robbed and killed him." I looked at Tre laying in the bed sleeping. I got up and walked to the bathroom.

"Do they know who did it?"

"Na. But I got word on the streets. 50K for information. If you hear anything let me know."

"I will." As I sat on the toilet, I hoped it wasn't Tre and Slim who killed my uncle, because he just told me he hit for a lot of money and dope.

I hoped and prayed it wasn't them because my uncle is crazy; he ain't to be played with and he was a real killer.

I walked out the bathroom, slid in the bed, wanting to ask him, but I needed to find out more information before I jumped to conclusion, because then I would have to choose between my family and my baby daddy.

***

Tre

When I got up the next evening, I looked at a photo on Michelle's phone. "Who's that?" I asked.

"My uncle."

"What he on?"

"I want to ask you something."

"What is it about?"

"You heard about someone killing a Jamaican in Kenner a couple days?"

"No, why you ask?"

"Well, because you told me you hit a lick. So, well, somebody went in my uncle's house and did a home invasion. Shit, you know how shit goes in the city."

"Yea, I know."

"I'm about to be out.

"I got something I want to tell you."

"What is it?"

"I'm pregnant."

"What! You got to get rid of it."

"I 'm not getting rid of shit."

"Fuck."

"And get out."

"What!"

"Fuck this shit! Get out my fucking house now."

"Motherfucker." I grabbed my gun, and keys and walked out.

I jumped in the car, pulling off with my head fucked up.

Chapter Thirty-One

Slim

I got up later on, looked over for Kim and she was gone. She must have went to work. I was glad because her ass act real fuck up when I didn't give her no dick. And I had been here a couple days.

I picked up my phone, looked at it, and scrolled down. I had a few missed calls from Len. I know she probably mad as a motherfucker because I told her I was coming through last night.

And I had a couple missed calls from a few of my white clientele I be serving grams to in the city and on the outskirts. I got up, walked in the bathroom, and hopped in the shower. I got out a few minutes later.

I walked in the room, put on some white Girbaud jeans shorts with my throwback Saints jersey, black Soulja Reeboks, and my fit black Saints hat.

I went in the clothes, grabbed a couple ounces of dope. I still had four bricks in the A/C vent along with my money. I had broken one key down. I grabbed my gun, keys and phone, and headed out the door.

I got in my truck, looked in the glove box, grabbing a bag of dope, snorting it and killing my morning sickness. The snorting was cool but I needed to hit that needle and get that good rush. I grabbed the blunt out the ashtray, lighting it up, taking a puff and blowing the smoke out my nose and mouth Then I pulled off with my head fucked up still thinking about last night. Nigga almost had the boy. I ain't heard from Trina either. I hope she made it.

I picked up the phone, dialing her number.

"Hello," a female said.

"Where Trina?"

"She in the hospital. She got shot at the club last night."

"Damn! She alright?"

"Yea, just got hit in the leg."

"Okay, tell her Slim called."

"Okay."

I hung up, hitting my blunt again shortly. I pulled up in the driveway, getting out the truck. I walked in the courtway. Rell, Tre and Craig was sitting on the porch talking, smoking weed.

"Damn! Nigga, when you got out?"

"Yesterday," Rell said, dapping me off.

"What's up, Tre and Craig?" I said, dapping them off.

"Nigga, you know us. Catching the morning rush."

"I got that for you," Craig said.

"Alright."

"Slim, throw a nigga something."

"I got you. Come."

"Slim, let me give that." I walked to his car. He gave the twenty grand."

"I need something else."

"I got you." I walked into Len house.

"Damn! Nigga, what happen to you last night?"

"Nigga almost killed my ass last night."

"What! Man, I don't know why you be fucking with them whole ass club chasing them dumb ass hood bitch."

"I need some work. Here, twenty thousand."

"You short."

"Yea, I took my cut."

"Here two ounces. I got to go get some more."

"Okay."

I walked outside.

"Tre, come take a ride with me." We jumped in the truck.

"What's up?" he said, hitting the blunt.

"Nigga try to kill my ass last night."

"What, where at?"

"At Xscape."

"Nigga, I told you them nigga out the eight looking to kill your ass."

"Damn! I forgot about that."

"Yea, the nigga named Death. He the one killed your nephew."

"Shit! I need to fuck him up."

"Yea, they said the nigga got a rep for killing niggas with a name."

"Okay, thanks, nigga." I dropped him off back in the project.

"I'm going to be back." I went home, grabbed a key and jumped back in my truck .

I sat in Len's house bagging up and breaking down. I gave Craig 4 half, gave Rell two ounce and 3000 grand. I put him on the team. The nigga Tricky hit me up talking about he need a ounces. He be hustling on Magnolia.

As I was standing in the driveway waiting for Tricky to pull up, my phone rang.

It was my brother from Angola.

"Woo. Nigga, what's up?"

"Nigga, you know the rodeo this weekend in."

"Okay. What you need me to bring?"

"A couple ounce of that dog food."

"Okay. I'ma bring you some money too."

"A'ight. Love you."

"Love you too." Tricky pulled up, stepped out his car. He followed me in the hallway. I served him a 4 way and got my money.

"Later, Slim."

"Later."

Just then my phone rang; it was my girl.

"You coming with me to the doctor appointment?"

"Yea."

"Okay. I'm going to meet you there."

I sat in the hospital room with her as they did the ultrasound showing us the baby.

"You see your little girl," Kim said, smiling.

"Yea," I said, smiling back at her."

"I'm going give you a picture. And give you your next appointment."

"Okay. Baby, we having a girl." I smiled, kissing her. "I love you."

"I love you back."

***

Slim

Tre, Craig, Rell and I jumped in the truck headed down St. Claude with AK-47 in the truck.

"We about to fuck everybody up out there," I said, passing the blunt to Tre.

"You know I'm with the fuck shit," he said, passing the blunt to Rell.

"Nigga, I just come home but you know I'm about this life," Rell said, passing the blunt.

"Let's do this shit," Craig said.

I turned on St. Rock, riding down. I don't see nobody. Then just round the corner—there they were, sitting on the step hustling with a bunch of niggas hanging out. With a lot of people outside.

I eased the window down and them niggas stuck the choppers out the window and went to hitting as I rode by. The bullets hit niggas, hoes and people. They went to running, ducking, screaming, grabbing their kids. Tre, Craig and Rell jumped out hitting the niggas on the set.

Tre shot a couple them niggas up. Rell shot a nigga that was trying to bust back. Craig was hitting at this Death who ran through the cut.

"Let's ride," I said.

They jumped in and I smashed out, heading uptown.

We stepped on the porch in the projects tooting dope and smoking a couple of blunts.

"Them niggas going to think twice about fucking with niggas out that wild Magnolia."

"For sure," they said, dapping each other off.

"You know we got to rep for that wild Magnolia," I said, smoking on a blunt."

Chapter Thirty-Two

Slim

Two weeks later, I was pulling up to Angola. I never thought I would see this motherfucker again. But every April and October they have a rodeo where the free people came and watch the rodeo as they ride horses, bulls and played other games. But niggas' family come and bring them drug and money and other shit.

It goes on for two weeks. Even though I don't like coming back up here, I couldn't let my brother down. Plus my mother wanted to come see him. My girl too and my nigga Tre. They never met my brother.

We walked up to the gate. The guard let us in. It was a big area in the back with benches and people walking around paying for things the inmates make up here, from belts to purses and wallets. And other things.

My brother spotted us and ran over to us, hugging and kissing my mother and dapping and hugging me.

I introduced him to my girl.

"Hey, pretty lady," he said, kissing her hand.

"Hey, how you doing? Nice to meet you."

"Same here."

"You big," my girl said.

"Yea, twenty-five years will get you this way."

"What's up, my nigga?" Tre said.

"Cool, I heard you my man right hand."

"Yea. It's all love."

"Come, Slim, let me holla at you." We walked to the back of the track where I gave him two ounces, 2,000 grand. Off that one key of dope I made three keys. That shit could take a seven; it was pure dope with no cut on it. I am glad that we hit the nigga Joe, for he'd never been stepped on. That's why me and Tre had the fire dope in the city.

"Thanks, little bro."

"That ain't shit." I watched as he handed off to somebody else.

Him and I walked the track talking.

"Nigga, I heard about you getting shot up. You need to slow down."

"Nigga, that shit easier said than done. Nigga, I don't do what I'm doing on the streets for nothing. You don't get this shit."

"I know. Damn! My nigga, just try and be cool, don't let no nigga steal you."

"I'm trying not to. My girl is having a baby. But nigga beef don't stop."

"That's why maybe you need to move."

"Nigga not running me nowhere."

"It's not about that; it's about being smart,."

"Well, my nigga, I love you and I'll think about it. But right now let's go enjoy this shit with mom."

"Okay. Love you," he said, hugging me tight.

We chilled, took pictures, watched him ride the bull and eat; we had a ball.

Chapter Thirty-Three

Slim

I was driving on the lakefront after I left from the Super Sunday.

I had a .45 on my lap with a bullet-proof vest on and a chopper in the back seat.

I was checking out a few hoes on the lake.

I pulled in the parking spot, stepping out the truck, looking at this big fine yellow bone chick with some blue short that had all her ass hanging out, with some blue fake weave hanging down to her ass.

Next thing I know, the fucking police was pulling up on me in three different cars. They just out pointing their guns.

"What's going on?"

"Put your hands in the air." I put my hands up as they walked up on me. One of them put me in handcuffs.

"Man, what did I do?"

"Yea, we been looking for you. For a couple months on a murder charge. Search the truck."

"Man, why y'all sweating!"

"Look, what we got—a chopper and some weed. Plus a .45 handgun. Plus it came back you got a warrant out for you on probation."

Damn! I'm fucked. They processed me into the Old Parish and booked me in a murder. And probation violation.

I called Kim. "Hello," she said.

"I'm back in jail."

"For what?"

"Murder and probation. And I can't bond out."

"Okay, I got you as always."

"Love you."

"Love you back.

I got off the phone. I couldn't believe I was back up in this bitch a day before my album was to come out.

"Man, my fuckin' luck fuck bad." I went and sat on my bunk. I know this bitch ass nigga was going to give me time. I just need to wait for him to come see me.

***

Two weeks later, I walked on visitation, sat at the booth. It was my P.O. I picked up the phone.

"Man, what's up?"

"I'm going to violate your parole and give you one year and a half; that way you'll be done with it when you get out. Good luck with the charge."

He hung up the phone and walked out.

I was glad he gave that and took me off paper. I don't need that shit no more in my life.

As I was about to get up, the C.O. told me I had another visit. I was waiting for my lawyer to come tomorrow. As I sat there he walked up; he picked up the phone.

"What's up? I thought you was coming tomorrow?"

"Yea, I was but the D.A. called and said they don't have enough to hold you, so you're free."

"Shit, but I saw the P.O. just came and gave me a year and half and took me off paper."

"Well, at least you won't be dealing with that shit no more."

"For sure. Later. Thanks for the help."

"You know I'm here. Good luck."

Chapter Thirty-Four

Tre

Six Months Later

I sat on the steps in the Nolia, watching these young niggas I be front dope to; they were serving dope fiends.

Rell and Craig get dope from me. But they be doing their own thing in the projects.

Tricky ass went back to jail on some beef shit for killing a nigga out the Fisher projects.

I still couldn't believe my nigga Slim was back upstate. His album had the city on fire as always but he never came home to see it through or to promote them. That nigga need to get that rapping shit up.

I got the project on smash with the heroin.

I met a connect out of New York. And be getting a few keys of dope cheap and be front to the young niggas in the projects and around the project on Phillip and Claire.

Just then my phone rang.

"Hello," Kim said.

"What's good?"

"Nigga, you suppose' to taking us to see Slim today."

"Damn! I forgot. I'm on my way."

"You got the stuff for him?"

"Yea, I got it. Bye." I pulled up to the apartment a couple minutes later. She was standing outside.

I handed her the stuff. She ran inside, putting it inside her pussy.

"You straight?" I asked

"Yea."

As we rode down I-10 headed to Allen Correctional Prison, my phone rang. I looked at it. It was Michelle. She had been blowing me up all day. I had stopped fucking with her after she told me she was pregnant and wasn't going to get abortion.

I hadn't talked to her in three weeks. I sent her ass to voicemail.

We walked into the visitation line, showed our ID's, and the C.O. walked us in the visitation where we were waiting on Slim to come out.

He walked out twenty minutes later.

He had on some blue jeans with *Allen Correctional* written down the legs in white, along with blue shirt with same thing written across the back, and black shining boots.

He walked up to me, dapping and hugging me.

"Man, thanks for bringing my girl."

"Nigga, you know I got you."

He walked over to Kim, kissing and hugging her.

"I love you."

"Love you back. Where you want me to bring this shit?"

"Bathroom, just drop it in the trash can." We watched as she went into the bathroom.

***

Michelle

I sat inside stressed the fuck out. This dumb ass nigga ain't answering. I been trying to call him and tell him my uncle found out he killed his brother and he looking to kill him and Slim. I been trying to give him a heads-up, but this stupid ass nigga won't answer his phone. He thinks I'm trying to break him and his girl up because I'm pregnant. I don't give a fuck about his girl. I ain't having no abortion. Just then my uncle called me.

"Hello," I said.

"You seen that nigga?"

"No, Uncle."

"Look, don't play with me."

"I ain't playing with you."

"That nigga killed my brother and I'm going to get his ass."

"Uncle, what about my baby?"

"You going to choose that nigga over the family?"

"So what I'm going to do? He's my kid's father."

176

"Look, I don't care about none of that. That nigga killed my brother."

"Whatever!" I hung up, dialing his number again.

Shit! Shit! The fucking voicemail. "You such a fucking asshole!" I said, hanging up the phone.

***

Tre

Before the visit was over, Slim pulled me to the side.

"What's good, my nigga?" I asked.

"I'm done with the streets."

"What! That's just the jail talking."

"Na, nigga, I'm done for real. My girl getting tired of this shit. I'm really get tired of this jail shit. I kicked the dope habit. It time for me the focus on this label. And I want you to be my partner."

"Shit, nigga, you know I'm down."

"Good. How shit been with you out there?"

"Shit been lovely. Got a connect out of New York. I'm running shit."

"Well, I'm going to need you to invest some of that money into this label."

"I got you."

"What up with Rell, Craig and Tricky?"

"Nothing, them niggas getting money. Tricky fighting a murder."

"Damn! What up with Len?"

"She send her love."

"Well, Kim talking about moving to Atlanta."

"Atlanta? What!"

"Yea, we just talking about it now."

"Visitation over!" the C.O. screamed.

"Think about what I said."

"I got you."

"Love you, Kim." He kissed her.

"Love you back."

As we drove down the interstate, I thought about my girl and son and I thought about Michelle. I know it was my baby. I couldn't leave her like that, knowing that's my baby.

I have to be there for my kids. I can't do what my father did me and my mother. I'm going to holla at her when I get back to the city. Besides, I was thinking about what Slim said to me. I might need to move around. The feds did put up the charges. I got five years' probation.

Len got off the charge.

So I need to count my blessings for real.

"What's on your mind?" Kim asked me."

"Huh?"

"You thinking hard."

"Yea, just about my life, that's all."

"Yea, you need to change. Me and Slim getting the fuck out of New Orleans. You and Sharon need to come with us."

"I know."

"I'm telling you. It going to be better than New Orleans."

"Yea, New Orleans all I know."

"Yea, try something different."

"You right. I'll think about it."

"Please do. Your girl really want to go." As I dropped Kim off home, my phone rang. It was Michelle.

"Hello."

"What kind of game you playing?" she said.

"Man, I'm going to be there for you and our kid."

"Nigga, I need to see you face to face. It's important."

"What up?"

"I can't tell you over the phone."

"Man, tell me. You been calling me all fucking day." Then I heard her start crying.

"Man, what wrong with you?"

"You killed my uncle."

"What! You tripping."

"No, I'm not." |

"Where you at?"

"In the project."

"Okay. I'm going to be through there in a couple hours."

"Okay. Bye."

***

Peter

I stood in the dark hallway waiting on this nigga to come see my niece with a .357 bull dog in my hand full of coke. I know he was going to come see her. Most niggas sucker for love. I know once I told her, she was going to warn the nigga.

She don't know she was bringing him to the lion to be eaten.

I'm a old school nigga. These young niggas out here killing for nothing. I been taking hits in New Orleans since the 70's. I did time in Angola and everything. That's how I met his cousin taking hits for him when he was selling weight back in the New Orleans in the early 90's.

But then I stopped and started getting work for me and lil' brother and got Kenner sold up with everything.

Now these young niggas thinking they were going to kill my brother and get away with it.

I was going to kill them, no matter what Luke said. And if he would have a problem with it, I was going to smoke his ass too.

That bitch Tracy lucky she dead, because I was going to make her pay dearly for fucking over my brother.

Bitch ain't shit. I had told him that when he was fucking the project bitch. Fuck that hoe and leave that bitch alone but he was pussy wipe.

Now he paying the price.

I watched as his car came in to the driveway. I was in the hallway across from my niece. I watched as she came downstairs and got in the car.

They was paying me no attention. I walked up to the car and before she could say shit, I blew his head off. Then I walked off in the dark project.

***

Michelle

I jumped out the car screaming and hollering with blood all over me. I couldn't believe my uncle just killed my baby daddy.

"Please! Please! Somebody help call 911." Everybody came out of their houses after the shooting, looking at me and at Tre's lifeless body and blood all over the car.

Just then the police came along with the ambulance. They made everybody back up. And put red and yellow tape up.

The ambulance removed Tre 's body from the car, trying to revive him, but it was too late.

The police came up to me asking me questions. I was still in shock but I couldn't rat on my uncle.

"Did you see what happened?" the white police officer asked me.

"No."

"What he had on?"

"I don't know. I heard somebody walked up to us and shot him in the head while we were talking."

"Did you get a look at him?"

"No."

"Okay. You free to go." I walked inside with my head fucked up. I got in the shower, letting the hot water rinse off my body. I was thinking about what just happened. I fell to the floor balling up, crying, thinking about I just lost my kid's father to my uncle. What in the fuck am I going to do?

Then it hit me. When Slim found out, he going to kill my ass thinking that I set his best friend up.

"Fuck! I'm stuck. Fuck!"

***

Sharon

I jumped in my car and rushed to the hospital with tears pouring down my face.

I was praying to God that he would live. I told his ass to get out of the game and let's move to another city because the streets of New Orleans never let go. I ran in the hospital, going to the nurse station. Then Kim ran in hugging me.

"Is Roosevelt Taylor here?"

"Yes, I'll go get the doctor." The doctor came out looking at me.

"I'm sorry he didn't make it"

"Please no. Please!" I said, falling to the floor.

Kim slid down to the floor, holding me.

"I got you."

It took me about an hour. I pulled myself together and went into the room where they had his body. They pulled the cover off so I could identify. He was lying there with two holes in his head swollen up. I broke down crying, leaning over on his body.

Kim pulled me off him, hugging me.

***

Slim

I sat in the visitation room waiting for Kim to walk in. She told me she had something to tell me and she needed to talk to me face to face. I had asked her several times to tell me, but she wouldn't.

Besides, she didn't sound right on the phone. I hope it wasn't nothing with the baby or my nigga Tre. I been calling that nigga phone but he ain't been answering.

She walked in with her hair in a ponytail and some blue jeans and yellow shirt with some tennis on, looking like she ain't slept in a couple of days. I knew then something was seriously wrong. I got up hugging and kissing her and she broke down crying in my arms.

"What is it, baby? Is it our daughter?"

She shook her head.

We walked over to the table sitting down. She took my hands inside of hers, rubbing them.

"What up?" I asked her.

"I got some bad news."

"What is it?"

"Tre dead."

"What!" I said, feeling some tears roll down my face.

"They found his body in his car in the Magnolia. He was shot twice in the head."

The only bitch I know he was fucking in Magnolia was the bitch Michelle. *That hoe set my dog up. I'm going to kill her when I get out*, I thought to myself.

"Look, I need you to holla at the lawyer, tell him we going to pay for everything and get help to enable me to come to the funeral."

"Okay. I'm on it."

"I love you."

"And I love you too."

One week later I was watching them put my right-hand man in the ground; it cost me $5000. I was there with two guards with guns, and I was shackled up.

My nigga didn't have an open casket.

They said he got shot close up with a .45 and they couldn't patch the hole up. I had tears streaming down my face thinking about all the good times we had together. And how we were supposed to start this label together.

I walked over to Sharon, hugged her and Tre's son who looked just like him.

"Slim, when you get out, kill the motherfucker who did this shit."

"Don't worry, I got this."

"Thank you," she said, walking off.

They let me stay and visit my family. I fucked my girl.

Then they took me back.

I guess when I get out I'm going to kill everything that had something to do with Tre's death.

I guess they are right: In the streets of New Orleans beef never dies.

To Be Continued—
The Streets Never Let Go 3
Coming Soon

Lock Down Publications and Ca$h Presents assisted publishing packages.

BASIC PACKAGE $499

Editing

Cover Design

Formatting

UPGRADED PACKAGE $800

Typing

Editing

Cover Design

Formatting

ADVANCE PACKAGE $1,200

Typing

Editing

Cover Design

Formatting

Copyright registration

Proofreading

Upload book to Amazon

LDP SUPREME PACKAGE $1,500

Typing

Editing

Cover Design

Formatting

Copyright registration

Proofreading

Set up Amazon account

Upload book to Amazon

Advertise on LDP Amazon and Facebook page

***Other services available upon request. Additional charges may apply

Lock Down Publications

P.O. Box 944

Stockbridge, GA 30281-9998

Phone # 470 303-9761

Submission Guideline

Submit the first three chapters of your completed manuscript to ldpsubmissions@gmail.com, subject line: Your book's title. The manuscript must be in a .doc file and sent as an attachment. Document should be in Times New Roman, double spaced and in size 12 font. Also, provide your synopsis and full contact information. If sending multiple submissions, they must each be in a separate email.

Have a story but no way to send it electronically? You can still submit to LDP/Ca$h Presents. Send in the first three chapters, written or typed, of your completed manuscript to:

LDP: Submissions Dept
Po Box 944
Stockbridge, Ga 30281

DO NOT send original manuscript. Must be a duplicate.

Provide your synopsis and a cover letter containing your full contact information.

Thanks for considering LDP and Ca$h Presents.

NEW RELEASES

BORN IN THE GRAVE by SELF MADE TAY
MOAN IN MY MOUTH by XTASY
SKI MASK MONEY by RENTA
C.R.E.A.M. 3 by YOLANDA MOORE
UNBREAK MY HEART by MIMI
SOUL OF A HUSTLER, HEART OF A KILLER by
SAYNOMORE
THE STREETS NEVER LET GO 3 by ROBERT BAPTISTE

Robert Baptiste

188

The Streets Never Let Go 2

STRAIGHT BEAST MODE III

De'Kari

KINGPIN KILLAZ IV

STREET KINGS III

PAID IN BLOOD III

CARTEL KILLAZ IV

DOPE GODS III

Hood Rich

SINS OF A HUSTLA II

ASAD

RICH $AVAGE II

By Martell Troublesome Bolden

YAYO V

Bred In The Game 2

S. Allen

THE STREETS WILL TALK II

By Yolanda Moore

SON OF A DOPE FIEND III

HEAVEN GOT A GHETTO II

SKI MASK MONEY II

By Renta

LOYALTY AIN'T PROMISED III

By Keith Williams

I'M NOTHING WITHOUT HIS LOVE II

SINS OF A THUG II

TO THE THUG I LOVED BEFORE II

IN A HUSTLER I TRUST II

By Monet Dragun

QUIET MONEY IV

EXTENDED CLIP III

Robert Baptiste

THUG LIFE IV
By **Trai'Quan**
THE STREETS MADE ME IV
By **Larry D. Wright**
IF YOU CROSS ME ONCE II
ANGEL IV
By **Anthony Fields**
THE STREETS WILL NEVER CLOSE IV
By K'ajji
HARD AND RUTHLESS III
KILLA KOUNTY III
By Khufu
MONEY GAME III
By Smoove Dolla
JACK BOYS VS DOPE BOYS II
A GANGSTA'S QUR'AN V
COKE GIRLZ II
COKE BOYS II
By Romell Tukes
MURDA WAS THE CASE II
Elijah R. Freeman
THE STREETS NEVER LET GO III
By Robert Baptiste
AN UNFORESEEN LOVE IV
By **Meesha**
KING OF THE TRENCHES III
by **GHOST & TRANAY ADAMS**

MONEY MAFIA II
By **Jibril Williams**
QUEEN OF THE ZOO III

The Streets Never Let Go 2

By **Black Migo**
VICIOUS LOYALTY III

By Kingpen
A GANGSTA'S PAIN III

By J-Blunt
CONFESSIONS OF A JACKBOY III

By Nicholas Lock
GRIMEY WAYS III

By Ray Vinci
KING KILLA II

By Vincent "Vitto" Holloway
BETRAYAL OF A THUG II

By Fre$h
THE MURDER QUEENS II

By Michael Gallon
THE BIRTH OF A GANGSTER III

By Delmont Player
TREAL LOVE II

By Le'Monica Jackson
FOR THE LOVE OF BLOOD II

By Jamel Mitchell
RAN OFF ON DA PLUG II

By Paper Boi Rari
HOOD CONSIGLIERE II

By Keese
PRETTY GIRLS DO NASTY THINGS II

By Nicole Goosby
PROTÉGÉ OF A LEGEND II

By Corey Robinson
IT'S JUST ME AND YOU II

Robert Baptiste

By Ah'Million
BORN IN THE GRAVE II
By Self Made Tay

<u>**Available Now**</u>

RESTRAINING ORDER **I & II**
By **CA$H & Coffee**
LOVE KNOWS NO BOUNDARIES **I II & III**
By **Coffee**
RAISED AS A GOON I, II, III & IV
BRED BY THE SLUMS I, II, III
BLAST FOR ME I & II
ROTTEN TO THE CORE I II III
A BRONX TALE I, II, III
DUFFLE BAG CARTEL I II III IV V VI
HEARTLESS GOON I II III IV V
A SAVAGE DOPEBOY I II
DRUG LORDS I II III
CUTTHROAT MAFIA I II
KING OF THE TRENCHES
By **Ghost**
LAY IT DOWN **I & II**
LAST OF A DYING BREED I II
BLOOD STAINS OF A SHOTTA I & II III
By **Jamaica**
LOYAL TO THE GAME I II III

LIFE OF SIN I, II III

By **TJ & Jelissa**

BLOODY COMMAS I & II

SKI MASK CARTEL I II & III

KING OF NEW YORK I II,III IV V

RISE TO POWER I II III

COKE KINGS I II III IV V

BORN HEARTLESS I II III IV

KING OF THE TRAP I II

By **T.J. Edwards**

IF LOVING HIM IS WRONG…I & II

LOVE ME EVEN WHEN IT HURTS I II III

By **Jelissa**

WHEN THE STREETS CLAP BACK I & II III

THE HEART OF A SAVAGE I II III IV

MONEY MAFIA

LOYAL TO THE SOIL I II III

By **Jibril Williams**

A DISTINGUISHED THUG STOLE MY HEART I II & III

LOVE SHOULDN'T HURT I II III IV

RENEGADE BOYS I II III IV

PAID IN KARMA I II III

SAVAGE STORMS I II III

AN UNFORESEEN LOVE I II III

By **Meesha**

A GANGSTER'S CODE I &, II III

A GANGSTER'S SYN I II III

THE SAVAGE LIFE I II III

CHAINED TO THE STREETS I II III

BLOOD ON THE MONEY I II III

Robert Baptiste

A GANGSTA'S PAIN I II
By J-Blunt
PUSH IT TO THE LIMIT
By **Bre' Hayes**
BLOOD OF A BOSS **I, II, III, IV, V**
SHADOWS OF THE GAME
TRAP BASTARD
By **Askari**
THE STREETS BLEED MURDER **I, II & III**
THE HEART OF A GANGSTA I II& III
By **Jerry Jackson**
CUM FOR ME I II III IV V VI VII VIII
An **LDP Erotica Collaboration**
BRIDE OF A HUSTLA **I II & II**
THE FETTI GIRLS **I, II& III**
CORRUPTED BY A GANGSTA I, II III, IV
BLINDED BY HIS LOVE
THE PRICE YOU PAY FOR LOVE I, II ,III
DOPE GIRL MAGIC I II III
By **Destiny Skai**
WHEN A GOOD GIRL GOES BAD
By **Adrienne**
THE COST OF LOYALTY I II III
By Kweli
A GANGSTER'S REVENGE **I II III & IV**
THE BOSS MAN'S DAUGHTERS I II III IV V
A SAVAGE LOVE **I & II**
BAE BELONGS TO ME I II
A HUSTLER'S DECEIT I, II, III
WHAT BAD BITCHES DO I, II, III

194

The Streets Never Let Go 2

SOUL OF A MONSTER I II III

KILL ZONE

A DOPE BOY'S QUEEN I II III

TIL DEATH

By **Aryanna**

A KINGPIN'S AMBITON

A KINGPIN'S AMBITION **II**

I MURDER FOR THE DOUGH

By **Ambitious**

TRUE SAVAGE I II III IV V VI VII

DOPE BOY MAGIC I, II, III

MIDNIGHT CARTEL I II III

CITY OF KINGZ I II

NIGHTMARE ON SILENT AVE

THE PLUG OF LIL MEXICO II

CLASSIC CITY

By **Chris Green**

A DOPEBOY'S PRAYER

By **Eddie "Wolf" Lee**

THE KING CARTEL **I, II & III**

By **Frank Gresham**

THESE NIGGAS AIN'T LOYAL **I, II & III**

By **Nikki Tee**

GANGSTA SHYT **I II &III**

By **CATO**

THE ULTIMATE BETRAYAL

By **Phoenix**

BOSS'N UP **I , II & III**

By **Royal Nicole**

I LOVE YOU TO DEATH

Robert Baptiste

By **Destiny J**
I RIDE FOR MY HITTA
I STILL RIDE FOR MY HITTA
By **Misty Holt**
LOVE & CHASIN' PAPER
By **Qay Crockett**
TO DIE IN VAIN
SINS OF A HUSTLA
By **ASAD**
BROOKLYN HUSTLAZ
By **Boogsy Morina**
BROOKLYN ON LOCK I & II
By **Sonovia**
GANGSTA CITY
By **Teddy Duke**
A DRUG KING AND HIS DIAMOND I & II III
A DOPEMAN'S RICHES
HER MAN, MINE'S TOO I, II
CASH MONEY HO'S
THE WIFEY I USED TO BE I II
PRETTY GIRLS DO NASTY THINGS
By Nicole Goosby
TRAPHOUSE KING **I II & III**
KINGPIN KILLAZ I II III
STREET KINGS I II
PAID IN BLOOD **I II**
CARTEL KILLAZ I II III
DOPE GODS I II
By **Hood Rich**
LIPSTICK KILLAH **I, II, III**

CRIME OF PASSION I II & III

FRIEND OR FOE I II III

By **Mimi**

STEADY MOBBN' **I, II, III**

THE STREETS STAINED MY SOUL I II III

By **Marcellus Allen**

WHO SHOT YA **I, II, III**

SON OF A DOPE FIEND I II

HEAVEN GOT A GHETTO

SKI MASK MONEY

Renta

GORILLAZ IN THE BAY **I II III IV**

TEARS OF A GANGSTA I II

3X KRAZY I II

STRAIGHT BEAST MODE I II

DE'KARI

TRIGGADALE I II III

MURDAROBER WAS THE CASE

Elijah R. Freeman

GOD BLESS THE TRAPPERS I, II, III

THESE SCANDALOUS STREETS I, II, III

FEAR MY GANGSTA I, II, III IV, V

THESE STREETS DON'T LOVE NOBODY I, II

BURY ME A G I, II, III, IV, V

A GANGSTA'S EMPIRE I, II, III, IV

THE DOPEMAN'S BODYGAURD I II

THE REALEST KILLAZ I II III

THE LAST OF THE OGS I II III

Tranay Adams

THE STREETS ARE CALLING

Robert Baptiste

Duquie Wilson
MARRIED TO A BOSS I II III
By Destiny Skai & Chris Green
KINGZ OF THE GAME I II III IV V VI
Playa Ray
SLAUGHTER GANG I II III
RUTHLESS HEART I II III
By Willie Slaughter
FUK SHYT
By Blakk Diamond
DON'T F#CK WITH MY HEART I II
By Linnea
ADDICTED TO THE DRAMA I II III
IN THE ARM OF HIS BOSS II
By Jamila
YAYO I II III IV
A SHOOTER'S AMBITION I II
BRED IN THE GAME
By S. Allen
TRAP GOD I II III
RICH $AVAGE
MONEY IN THE GRAVE I II III
By Martell Troublesome Bolden
FOREVER GANGSTA
GLOCKS ON SATIN SHEETS I II
By Adrian Dulan
TOE TAGZ I II III IV
LEVELS TO THIS SHYT I II
IT'S JUST ME AND YOU
By Ah'Million

The Streets Never Let Go 2

KINGPIN DREAMS I II III
RAN OFF ON DA PLUG
By Paper Boi Rari
CONFESSIONS OF A GANGSTA I II III IV
CONFESSIONS OF A JACKBOY I II
By Nicholas Lock
I'M NOTHING WITHOUT HIS LOVE
SINS OF A THUG
TO THE THUG I LOVED BEFORE
A GANGSTA SAVED XMAS
IN A HUSTLER I TRUST
By Monet Dragun
CAUGHT UP IN THE LIFE I II III
THE STREETS NEVER LET GO I II
By Robert Baptiste
NEW TO THE GAME I II III
MONEY, MURDER & MEMORIES I II III
By **Malik D. Rice**
LIFE OF A SAVAGE I II III
A GANGSTA'S QUR'AN I II III IV
MURDA SEASON I II III
GANGLAND CARTEL I II III
CHI'RAQ GANGSTAS I II III
KILLERS ON ELM STREET I II III
JACK BOYZ N DA BRONX I II III
A DOPEBOY'S DREAM I II III
JACK BOYS VS DOPE BOYS
COKE GIRLZ
COKE BOYS
By Romell Tukes

Robert Baptiste

LOYALTY AIN'T PROMISED I II

By Keith Williams

QUIET MONEY I II III

THUG LIFE I II III

EXTENDED CLIP I II

By **Trai'Quan**

THE STREETS MADE ME I II III

By **Larry D. Wright**

THE ULTIMATE SACRIFICE I, II, III, IV, V, VI

KHADIFI

IF YOU CROSS ME ONCE

ANGEL I II III

IN THE BLINK OF AN EYE

By **Anthony Fields**

THE LIFE OF A HOOD STAR

By Ca$h & Rashia Wilson

THE STREETS WILL NEVER CLOSE I II III

By K'ajji

CREAM I II III

THE STREETS WILL TALK

By Yolanda Moore

NIGHTMARES OF A HUSTLA I II III

By King Dream

CONCRETE KILLA I II III

VICIOUS LOYALTY I II

By Kingpen

HARD AND RUTHLESS I II

MOB TOWN 251

THE BILLIONAIRE BENTLEYS I II III

By Von Diesel

200

GHOST MOB

Stilloan Robinson

MOB TIES I II III IV V VI

SOUL OF A HUSTLER, HEART OF A KILLER

By SayNoMore

BODYMORE MURDERLAND I II III

THE BIRTH OF A GANGSTER I II

By Delmont Player

FOR THE LOVE OF A BOSS

By C. D. Blue

MOB$ED UP I II III IV

THE BRICK MAN I II III IV

THE COCAINE PRINCESS I II III IV V

By King Rio

KILLA KOUNTY I II III

By Khufu

MONEY GAME I II

By Smoove Dolla

A GANGSTA'S KARMA I II

By FLAME

KING OF THE TRENCHES I II

by **GHOST & TRANAY ADAMS**

QUEEN OF THE ZOO I II

By **Black Migo**

GRIMEY WAYS I II

By Ray Vinci

XMAS WITH AN ATL SHOOTER

By Ca$h & Destiny Skai

KING KILLA

By Vincent "Vitto" Holloway

Robert Baptiste

BETRAYAL OF A THUG
By Fre$h
THE MURDER QUEENS
By Michael Gallon
TREAL LOVE
By Le'Monica Jackson
FOR THE LOVE OF BLOOD
By Jamel Mitchell
HOOD CONSIGLIERE
By Keese
PROTÉGÉ OF A LEGEND
By Corey Robinson
BORN IN THE GRAVE
By Self Made Tay
MOAN IN MY MOUTH
By XTASY

<u>BOOKS BY LDP'S CEO, CA$H</u>

TRUST IN NO MAN

TRUST IN NO MAN 2

TRUST IN NO MAN 3

BONDED BY BLOOD

SHORTY GOT A THUG

THUGS CRY

THUGS CRY 2

THUGS CRY 3

TRUST NO BITCH

TRUST NO BITCH 2

TRUST NO BITCH 3

TIL MY CASKET DROPS

RESTRAINING ORDER

RESTRAINING ORDER 2

IN LOVE WITH A CONVICT

LIFE OF A HOOD STAR

XMAS WITH AN ATL SHOOTER

Robert Baptiste

www.ingramcontent.com/pod-product-compliance
Lightning Source LLC
Chambersburg PA
CBHW070503260626
47161CB00004B/1441